6

por la

que merecen mi vida.

María

11 - XII - 2005

GW00838876

Center for Basque Studies
Basque Literature Series, No. 2

BASQUE LITERATURE SERIES

M.L. OÑEDERRA

And the Serpent Said to the Woman

Translated from Basque by
Kristin Addis

Basque Literature Series Editors
Mari Jose Olaziregi and Linda White

Center for Basque Studies,
University of Nevada, Reno

Center for Basque Studies
Basque Literature Series, No. 2

Center for Basque Studies
University of Nevada, Reno
Reno, Nevada 89557
http://basque.unr.edu

Copyright © 2005 by the Center for Basque Studies
M.L. Oñederra's *And the Serpent Said to the Woman* was originally
published as *Eta emakumeari sugeak esan zion* by Erein Publishing
House (Basque Country-Spain) © 1999.
Copyright © M.L. Oñederra 1999
English translation: Kristin Addis © 2005.
Text edited by Peter Holm-Jensen.
All rights reserved. Printed in the United States of America.

Series design © 2005 by Jose Luis Agote.
Cover design by Jose Luis Agote.

ISBN 1-877802-58-1

Acknowledgments

The translation of these stories was made possible by funding from the Basque Government, in collaboration with the Ministry of Education, Universities and Research, the Ministry of Culture, and the Secretary General of Foreign Affairs.

To Antonio

there is no Paradise
there is no hereafter

no future
keine Zukunft

they didn't tell us the truth
there is no other level

you are not getting bigger
you are aging

we are not preparing ourselves for anything
preparation is life

there is nothing but preparation
there is no goal

we are not arriving anywhere
we are passed by

they have passed
they will pass

hours and days
days and months

months and seasons
years

panta rhei
and there is no goal

there is no arriving anywhere
there is nothing to arrive at
the only arrival is death,
in the meantime there is nothing to arrive at

fleeting footholds,
essential excuses

the names of illusions,
words

there is always the word
the word remains even from those who have
crossed over

words and names,
the idea of holding onto something

name time
hours and days

days and months
months and seasons

Jasper Johns,
the four seasons

or Antonio Vivaldi
le quattro stagioni

i musici,
il cimento dell'armonia e dell'invenzione

De André
passerà anche questa stazione
this season too shall pass,
senza far male
doing no harm

passerà questa pioggia sottile
and the rain,
the rain too shall pass

come passa il dolore
pain,
as pain passes

as it passes
as
it ends

will it pass
will pain
end

pain,
pain left behind by long-gone times

Juliet,
when we made love,
you used to cry

DIRE STRAITS, *Romeo and Juliet*

Your childhood memories have started to fade into the distance like the mountains around the airport, and a fearsome hole is opening up inside you.

What was it that happened when you were looking out the window of the Deba-San Sebastián bus, at the stop in Itziar, perhaps? You would have been about twenty. What was it that happened to make you remember that day, that moment, every time you've leaned your head against the glass window of a vehicle since then?

In old age, childhood memories are said to return, filling the heads of the oldest people until there's no room left to remember what they did today. But that will be another age. If it is to be. If there is to be an old age for you. He, Andrés, the man at your side, your husband, he will have an elegant old age, ordered and lush. You don't know, don't know if you'll be together then, don't know if you'll even have word of one another. You don't think he'll need you. If you're not there, he won't need you. You know, if you are there, that he'll love you, calmly, he'll love you in his own way, and maybe by then you won't need anything more. It will be enough for you, maybe, his calm love. You don't know. Maybe, maybe it will be like that then.

During the years, those ten years that you spent together in the town you left only a few hours ago, perhaps you got bored. Even though you tried to do many things, made an effort to be different, you began to worry that the daily grind would eat away at you both. You had always thought they were dead, those people who always lived in the same town, with the same friends, those tidy people who never departed from the same old ways and habits. Life is about discovering the hidden, about discovering unknown intimate fears, about feeling. That's what life is, and everything else, even in the best of cases, is just a half-life. A bit false. Boring, at least for anyone looking on. But maybe you also fell into the trap. Perhaps there is no other way.

About one thing there's no doubt. You didn't get bored, and you weren't boring either. Never. Not you, and not Andrés. No, Andrés surely didn't get bored either. Not either one of you on your own but both of you together, maybe. Or at least, something has grown dull. Fighting this, fleeing this, is probably why you're so tired, probably because of this you feel so trapped by the incredible exhaustion that weighs heavier from day to day. So many years fleeing boredom, afraid of becoming boring. Too many years.

Because of this, because you're so very tired, you're going abroad with him. Abroad, for a change. With him, because you don't have the strength to go alone or stay alone. You want to leave your beloved suffocating milieu for a whole year. A parenthesis, a twelve-month parenthesis. You think your exhaustion will be cured by being away from your work and your environment for a year.

You don't know now that in a year, your exhaustion will be greater. Too great to bear. So great that a strength you don't now have will arise from somewhere inside you. Now you come to the city by plane, but then you'll leave by train. You are coming with your husband, but you'll leave alone.

You don't know now that the parenthesis you are opening will never again close on its own.

Now you're going. That's what you know now, your present truth. You're going abroad. Away, for a year. Most likely, you'll even want to return. Want to go home. Homesickness. You don't know. You'd like to feel that again sometime. To fall in love again also. If it's possible to fall in love again. It's more likely that you'll feel homesick again. If you spend enough time away from home, you might get homesick. Homesickness. Whatever that is. Like when you used to go to England in the summers when you were young. That might have been homesickness. Or when they sent you to camp as a kid. If camp was far enough away to call that homesickness. Homesickness. Lovesickness. At the moment at least, you're very tired.

Too tired to realize that going away won't take you away, away from yourself. This foreign country is Luis and Luis isn't outside you, but a part of you, an intimate part, with you for a very long time, wrapped up in your roots. You'll have to get a lot more tired, you'll have to endure the silent exhaustions of a full year to realize this, to realize even this.

A full year in an unfamiliar town, in a new house, with two people you've known for a long time, in order to stand being alone at last. To go. To flee. Long stories hold no secrets for those who listen to them. For those who live them, yes. For those who live them, stories are always short. The unbearable fatigue of a large accumulation of small moments. To know how it ends, it has to play out. You have to play it out.

You're very tired and you realize that you're about to arrive when the stewardess announces that the descent has begun and that seatbelts must be fastened. You have almost no strength. Your fatigue is increased by the mere thought that you'll have to talk to Luis, who by now is waiting for you in the airport. You're thinking about the minimum required by common courtesy. How's it going, it's been a while. What common courtesy requires, what it provides. Thank God for stock phrases. Hello, how are you. Hi, what's up. Stock phrases requiring no thought, the ones courtesy hands us already complete. No, you won't be capable. Why doesn't the airplane take another turn? Nerves, fear of seeing Luis again after so many years, a stranger after the long silence between you. He might have changed a lot. A stranger because of distance. The power of time and place.

The time when childhood memories start to fade into the distance, you wrote to Luis in the letter telling him you had to come to W. with your husband. Find us a comfortable place, please, and don't worry too much about the price. The contract Andrés had with the UN would give him a good wage.

Luis knows that your husband is an economist or something like that. And that his name is Andrés. Andrés, that tall clever guy you married. He thinks he saw him once or twice, at a friend's wedding or something. He has never spoken with him. At first, because he was your husband. Later, because he just didn't bother. Finally, for lack of opportunity since he, Luis, left the Basque Country twelve years ago or more.

Luis phoned to say that there was plenty of room at his house.

When you talked on the phone that time, the time Luis called you to answer your letter, your voice, which he hadn't heard for years, was less familiar to him than he expected. A year ago. Or so.

It was really two apartments that had been joined at some point and, at least if you didn't mind sharing a kitchen, you would have plenty of space and independence. It wasn't easy, otherwise, to find a place in downtown W. It was in a good location. There were metro stations and streetcar stops within two minutes of the house. He sometimes walked to the university. You would help him pay the rent; it wasn't too expensive, but since he was alone now, it was harder for him to pay it than before.

At the time, Luis didn't confess even to himself his revived curiosity about you, his sudden desire to see you again. He didn't deny it either. He didn't think about it. He stored it away in some secret place within himself.

You, you again: when you were young, when you were students, way back then, as if something had been left hanging between you.

At the airport, waiting for the plane that would bring you and your husband, something akin to fear swept over Luis for a second when he remembered your voice; not the voice he heard on the telephone that last time, but the long-ago voice, Teresa's voice, breaking into laughter at some silly thing he said.

He decided to get a coffee, since the plane wouldn't arrive for another twenty minutes. And then you'd have to get your suitcases. Does he have the right to have you stay with him? Does he want to see you for a year in his home with another man? Has time passed, have the years passed, or is he still the one who would walk to the end of the pier with you on Sundays? That same guy. Coffee paid for, newspaper folded, he sets off for international arrivals. When he stops by a post at an appropriate distance to be able to see everyone coming through the automatic door, the load of the years that have passed suddenly calms him down.

The last passengers of one plane are dribbling out, or the first of another. They come out one by one. Little by little a crowd gathers, and with a single opening of the automatic door twenty or so all come out together, one right after another. Luis' heart leaps and his mouth dries. No, it's not you. That woman is fifty years old, and doesn't look anything like you anyway. Her short hair and jeans fooled him. But to tell the truth, Luis doesn't know how you wear your hair now, or if you ever wear jeans. He didn't ask you anything like that when you were talking on the phone. You only talked about the house and the dates. No, a bit about politics too, nothing important. Apparently things haven't changed much, there doesn't seem to be much going on that he can't find out from the newspapers. In some places there's almost nothing worth telling going on. In others, in yours, the same old stories are told again and again, as if time never advanced.

There, yes. You, Teresa. A large dark jacket and a long black skirt. The hair short, but not as short as Luis had imagined, and rather wavy besides. White tennis shoes give you a strange look. Your face looks like you just got out of bed, like you just got up after not sleeping well. At your side, pushing a luggage cart, your tall, clever husband.

As you approach, the lemony smell of a penetrating perfume reaches somewhere deeper than Luis' sense of smell. You look younger than he thought, very close to the

Teresa he remembered. You've changed less than he thought, but you look like you've seen a few things, many things. You've lost weight. Because you've lived through more than a few mornings like this, it doesn't seem likely that you'll comment overmuch on your sleepiness or the weather. A sweet smile without the slightest hint of passion and two kisses. Your lips don't touch Luis' cheek.

"How are you, Luis? Andrés, my husband."

Maybe you were always like that. The two men smile at each other and shake hands. Luis says they can leave the luggage cart in the parking lot when they get the car. Then Andrés, saying *avanti!*, pushes the cart and sets off for the corridor to the parking lot that Luis pointed out. Andrés' voice seems very loud to Luis. Andrés' voice, Andrés' movements. But he also likes the pants Andrés is wearing. Did you buy them for him?

You're the last to reach the car. You come along behind the two men, looking at all the postcard shops, ads and signs. You've started to try out the new language to yourself. You're making up sentences with the grammar you memorized, the words you're reading. Luis has surely noticed. You wrote him that you were taking an intensive course. Yes, in an academy close to home, surrounded by spoiled kids looking for their first job. That's how you put it in the letter. Wanting to be funny. Now you just don't want to look bad in front of him.

In the meantime, Andrés has asked Luis about the weather, and Luis has asked about the flight. The price of parking and the payment system, how far away the car is, he thought it was closer, but these buildings are deceptive, yes, he came in through a different door. There, at last, the car, red, Luis' rather dirty red car.

Andrés gets into the back seat. Luis starts the car.

You put on your seatbelt and look at Luis with the look of someone telling a serious joke. "I prefer to wear it," you say, almost under your breath, as if you were talking to yourself, looking straight ahead. Then you look out the right-hand window.

It appears you have no intention of wasting time on worthless trivialities. To tell the truth, that's the impression Luis has had of you since he met you. You behave properly. You do the right thing. You wear your seatbelt. Then you retreat; you disappear into your own world. Luis has never thought this was a bad thing. It's almost attractive.

Exhaustion, eternal exhaustion fills your insides and chills your hands. W. will be a break, after giving over almost your whole life to trying to find friends in your lovers and lovers among your friends. It's raining and the streets glimmer. It's pretty to arrive in a strange town in the rain. The night seems closer. You don't feel that foreign. The foreignness of the city doesn't seem that harsh to you.

How easy it was for the magazine to give permission, they'll get along without you easily. Besides, once a month or so you'll send articles, cultural chronicles. In W. there's plenty to tell about. You have a collection of stories inside you, a novel, a hidden intention to try to write something. Fiction has long tempted you, you're bored with always commenting on what others have done. You're bored and, above all, there's that exhaustion. You don't know if you'll be capable. You don't know if you'll dare. If you'll have the strength.

Maybe they'll have to get along without you forever. This year's leave of absence will stretch out, you'll stretch it out, even if you don't know it, sometimes the shadow of worry about illness that covers you silent as mist darkens your thoughts about the future. You even talked to the doctor about this before you came. He told you you needed to relax. To relax, that's all. The way you live your life, nothing was surprising, not your exhaustion, not your headaches, not even your period jumping around. That was the least of your worries.

The car goes on, as if by itself. Luis doesn't talk much; neither does anyone else.

Maybe you did something wrong, confused something, went too far in search of something. In search of what? In search of whom? In search of someone. Someone else. Someone not there. Someone, something that's not there, that's nowhere in the world. Fooled, condemned to eternal searching, since what is not there can never be found. A punishment for having eaten the forbidden fruit. From then on, Eve was unable to touch Adam's soul. His skin, yes, his skin and his saliva. Adam's hair. Adam's penis. But she never again touched his soul, and Eve, even when she was with Adam, even when making love or giving birth, Eve felt alone. Yes, maybe that was the punishment, the sentence handed down for having eaten the forbidden fruit. Maybe one has to accept it to have peace. Stop searching. Desist. Relax. Where exactly is the border between calm and solitude, after all? Give in. Desist. Stop searching for Adam's soul. Forget about wanting to touch another. Give in to solitude, give it room. Accept it.

That exhaustion. What will you write your novel about? You can't understand what's happening to you, why you're always tired, why you're tired all over. You would like to write about love. Clean out your brain as if it were a closet. You're even tired of Andrés, you can't stand his touch but if he doesn't touch you for a long time, you feel like he doesn't love you enough. Maybe he doesn't love you at all. Maybe it's true that love comes to an end and maybe the love between you has come to an end.

You should write about the end of love. About whatever is left.

Is there anything left? Or does love go from passion to calm and only passion is called love? What comes next, the calm that comes next, that other season of love, has no name. Love, adoration. Said together they don't seem to mean the same thing. Meaning full, meaningful, meaning. Wittgenstein. Where are you, Wittgenstein?

Young Imanol who works for the magazine writing about rock concerts didn't know who Wittgenstein was. Ah, Imanol. You felt a fierce desire to touch his hand, a raw desire to touch Imanol's hand when he passed you the coffee, saying that he didn't know who Wittgenstein was. You wanted to strangle the desire to touch the skin of his hand with the tip of your finger, when you told him Wittgenstein went crazy because he knew too much about language. Why didn't you ask for his address? You won't write to him at the magazine to confess that you want to dream about his glance. How could you write that to him? What are you thinking? You are, you're supposed to be, a grown woman, married, balanced, fulfilled. Supposed to be. Let it be so.

Once in a while, Andrés asks something about a building, or about a street, or if they're going north. Luis explains the district's numbering system, like an onion, the districts that surround the central area, chaining it in, superimposed on one another. He lives in the ninth district. The first is the city center: the opera, the cathedral and things like that are in it. Yes, Andrés, like most tourists, has seen it before, he doesn't know how many years ago, when he spent a couple of days here on the way back from Prague. Silence again.

You remember that trip of Andrés'. You had a lot of work to do and you didn't go with him. Come with him. Not then, but now, yes.

A long silence. Yet no one seems uncomfortable. The car wheels make a continuous whoosh on the wet streets. In the car, your dry lemon perfume mixes with something else. You can feel the heater, and the windows have started to steam up. Luis says they're almost home, but nobody seems to be in much of a hurry.

A winter's journey comes to Andrés' mind, a trip somewhere with you in the winter, or trips, since he has often traveled in a car with you. Winter and summer with you, with your smell in the car. But the one knocking around inside his head was in the winter. Winter light, or the heat of the car, or the smell of your perfume warmed by the heater.

The street is wet and Luis drives well, smoothly. Luis, bachelor. He, married, married to you. Luis told you he was alone, he was alone now, he's ended up alone. That means that until now, until just now, there was someone, he wasn't alone. The wet streets, the shine of the asphalt and, farther on, farther to the left, water, a wide unshining canal that crosses the gray city, the urban stone bridges that cross the canal. You talked to Luis and you arranged the house between the two of you. It's OK, it's OK for somebody to take charge of things.

As soon as he gets settled in, Andrés will have to start working on various matters at the job he has to start tomorrow. He's eager to start his new job, even though he doesn't know exactly what it will be like. Because he doesn't know, most likely.

You're also looking out the window, but to the right. You must not be able to see the canal. You, Teresa, his wife. The calm of the word wife is lost to Andrés in the steam on the windows, he's thinking that he wrote down the telephone number they gave him for work in his appointment book.

The little girl who rode with her parents in the car comes
to your mind. The car crosses the city
almost gliding on the whoosh of the tires
in the puddles on the road
in the calm of a Saturday afternoon.

The husband of one of your mother's cousins died. Your father
says they have funerals early in the villages;
in San Sebastián they're at dusk. But
that way they'll get home earlier and
still have time to do something else.
What does your father have to do? What do
fathers do when they're neither at work
nor at home? Today your father didn't take a nap.

The little girl looks out the car window
at the rainy landscape.
"What a sad town. What's it called?"

"Alegria. Happiness. Alegria de Oria."

You remember your mother's smile, your mother's
smile as she turned from her seat in the front
to look at you in the back. Your mother's
gaze. Yes? Do you remember? Her voice?
Really? Your mother's face? Your mother,
who answered you laughing? No, you remember
the gray of the gray streets of that town, the rain.

You remember your amazement, your
solitude, how could they have given a name like that
to that town, didn't it seem sad, incredibly sad,
to anyone else? By now your mother and father
are talking about something else in the front seat.
They've forgotten about you, the little girl in the back seat,
and that little girl was left alone in the back
with her unbearable amazement,
with her sad amazement.

You remember your amazement, the amazement
that is still with you. The amazement and the solitude.
Your smallness, your impotence in the face of the
names people give towns. That's what remains with you.
That's why you know, you think, that that little girl
on her way to the funeral of an uncle she never knew
was you. Is you.

Fall
Udazkena
Automne
Otoño
Autumn
Herbst
Ngahuru
Ašun
Varsha
Quitian
Aki

Saturday, 5:00 pm

Cuando incluso la nostalgia me ha abandonado, you wrote on a yellow piece of paper. From time to time you come up with a sentence like that and you have to write it down, your internal explosion from breast to arm, from arm to hand, drawn down to your fingertips, through the ink, as if you spilled it out into the letters on the paper.

You look out the window. The first leaves of autumn have started to fall. What happens to you on damp fall afternoons in San Sebastián has started to happen to you in W. too. That chill that sinks from your sternum, slides between your breasts. A draft that tightens your breath and roils your gut.

So it wasn't San Sebastián then. It might be fall, but not any fall and not any moment. Throughout your

whole life, your time, throughout your whole time, things
coming to an end have made you like this. Soft. Weak.
Sensitive. Overflowing with sadness. Things left hanging
for a long time, left behind somewhere, unfinished,
unclosed. The pieces of life you've left open, waiting.
Looking out the window in autumn dusk, for example.
You haven't looked out the window for ages. No, for years
you haven't looked, just looked. It's a break. Nothingness
which begins at some lost point of memory. All the time
you've spent not looking out the window is a black hole.
Nothingness. And breaking the nothingness is to begin
looking out the window again, when the first leaves of
autumn begin to fall. For the first time in a long time. To
look for the first time in a long time and see the leaves
falling.

Autumn, dampness, wet rotting leaves and the world,
history, life. You don't know where to begin thinking to be
able to escape this glutted sensation that suffocates you.
You turn your gaze to the other side of the room, let it
creep over the furniture and the carpet, and you see your
husband in the yellow light of the floor lamp. You see him
sitting there, reading, living, his hand dangling over the
arm of the chair, in all his glory. This is life, this is how
individual history materializes from day to day, from hour
to hour, from minute to minute. Your husband, your
man, a man, not single, yours. You know that you were
not your husband's first woman, nor will you be the last.
You know this or you want it. What do you know of your
husband? The magnetism of risk. The attraction of fear.
Some men, some other men, marry the first woman they
like. Then reinforce their choice by despising any appeal-
ing women they meet in later years. Life. Ways of life.

Responses to fear.

Andrés hasn't seen you so calm for a long time, so still. Being in other people's houses must give you this calm, the time to look out the window. At home you always have something to do, something to put away, something to clean, things to do, when you're at home.

Here you spend more time in the house, you're foreigners and you don't know anybody. All the same, you don't feel much like going out. When you planned the trip, there were so many museums and films you would see, and theater, what better way to learn German well than to see things you already knew, in German. So you said to Andrés with great certainty. You were justifying coming with him. Rationalizing. Giving him reasons to believe you. But now you don't feel much like going out. Not at the moment. Well, you've only been there a short time, you'll get used to it. You don't even write much and that's the only thing that keeps you calm at home. No, you don't even write letters. You don't do anything. You exist. You have no strength for anything. Even existing tires you, but this fatigue doesn't hurt. It pulls you in. You've begun to feel comfort in fatigue.

Today, for example, you've spent a half an hour or more looking out the window.

Andrés doesn't know for sure how much time you've spent looking out the window, he's lost track. Yes, the last time he looked up from his newspaper, you were looking out the window and it must have been half an hour since then, he reckons, because he's read a couple of articles almost all the way through.

Andrés is content because he has time to read the newspaper, to relax and read the whole newspaper. At last, a comfortable job, just for a year, but comfortable. And what's more, it doesn't look like it's going to change. At most, a hop to Brussels. A couple of days. Get on an airplane and go, get on an airplane and come back. He, his world, his airplanes. You, your world, your silences.

He hasn't yet taken a trip on his own since you've been in W. You've never yet stayed alone, without Andrés, with Luis, for a few days, the two of you alone at home. It will happen. That too will happen. It will happen when it happens.

You stand up, start to leave the window and it seems to Andrés that you're going to leave the room. Purposeful steps, the gait of someone who has reached a clear decision. When you pass before Andrés, you don't even look at him. He, just in case, had prepared something to say, something stupid, to tell the truth. "What, in search of inspiration?" or some similar nonsense. It's always better, with you, to say something rather than to remain silent. With you, with this latest Teresa. Because you're saddened by silent glances, you get sad if someone looks at you and doesn't say anything. Andrés has gotten used to answering automatically. He's gotten the hang of it lately. Anything not to end up stark naked in the face of your long, deep, incomprehensible sadness.

Can coming to W. cure you, will it cure you? Changes are always good. Nevertheless, Andrés doesn't want to worry too much. He blanks out the images evoked by the word cure without examining them too closely. It must be your age, he thinks. He thinks he'll never have age problems, but women are different. Besides, age problems, crises, supposedly come earlier to women.

Best to stay silent without shutting up.

Wives, types of married women. Wives who don't work. For example. Not like you. The wives of some of

Andrés' colleagues. Active men, men of ideas, economists, professionals, and their trophy wives, who prepare dinners, who fill their daily lives with creams and massages. No, you're not like that. Even if you stopped working altogether (is that what's running through your mind?) you wouldn't be like that. You use makeup less and less, it seems to Andrés, you're more and more colorless. Nevertheless, does Andrés want a trophy wife? Even if he hasn't said so, he has always been quite proud of his wife, not as a trophy, but exactly what you are he would find hard to say (and if you stopped working in order to assist him?). The model couple he saw at that lecture comes to his mind. It was the husband who gave the lecture, but the wife, the great woman behind the great man, was there, silent but wise. She was there. The husband mentioned her in his lecture, saying she was his best and most indispensable assistant. The wife gave a beatific smile and some members of the audience clapped. Everybody smiled. Andrés is disgusted by the memory, but the speaker was an acquaintance of his boss at work and he smiled too. The lecture wasn't bad, but he hardly remembers the content. He remembers the washed-out wife. *The sad appearance of smooth management and accepted dependency.* They could have been your words. When you wanted to be funny, when you were with people you could make laugh, you would say things like that. It seemed to Andrés that your words made people laugh—you made him laugh and it pleased him that you also made other people laugh.

When you were in the mood for it.

Will you ever be again?

Yes, you've gone to the kitchen. Luis is there, he seems to be there, there's noise.

Your burst of laughter.

Andrés likes to hear you laugh, even if you're with someone else. You laugh very little with him lately. And he doesn't laugh much with you. He doesn't get on too badly with Luis, sometimes even laughs with him. Luis is new, new and pleasant company. It was a good idea to come with you to Luis' house, even if something draws a question mark inside him.

But Andrés doesn't want to think about that. Better not to think about it. Even if he thinks a lot, things will happen just the same, they will happen.

He looks at the portrait of Arafat in the newspaper, always with that cloth on his head and in military dress. How ugly Arafat is. Arafat. Arabs. Monday's meeting comes to mind and he plunges himself into the newspaper again.

Saturday, 5:05 pm

When you enter the kitchen, Luis is putting some things he bought at the supermarket in the refrigerator.

"Do you remember Andoni?" you ask by way of greeting, leaning on the doorframe.

"Yes," Luis answers with a mischievous smile. "I was very jealous when you fell in love with him."

A loud nervous laugh escapes you. "I don't know if I fell in love or was just taken in."

"It's the same thing, isn't it? If you're ready to fall in love, you fall in love. You let yourself be taken in." Luis, standing, closes the refrigerator door. He sits on the edge of a low cupboard and takes his cigarettes out of his pocket. He offers you one.

"I don't know, but who cares." You light your cigarette on the match Luis holds out to you. You feel lost.

You don't know why you started talking about Andoni, but you did start, and now you have to continue.

"Last year his son called me. He's eighteen, well, by now he must be nineteen. He called me at work, I'd never spoken with him before. I never even met him, but I knew who he was immediately, as soon as he said his name. Andoni talked so much about him, Jon this and Jon that. Jon Ibaizabal, Andoni's son. Do you know why he called me?" Luis looks curious. "Because he didn't know what to do about his father, his father was sick and he didn't know what to do. At first I couldn't even answer him. I thought something must be very wrong if Andoni's son was calling me. I think I was still imagining a little kid, as if time hadn't passed, and there he was, the kid, asking me to go see his father, because he thought it would be a good thing, he knew I'd been important to his father. That little kid, saying he knew I'd been important in his father's life."

With your expression, with your tone, you try to show the detachment of the disbeliever.

You go over and sit at Luis' side, on his left, your bottom on the edge of the cupboard. Luis is looking down, his left arm crossed across his belly, the other stretched out, cigarette in hand, held between his pointer and middle fingers.

"Is that why you said that thing about childhood memories when you wrote to me? Don't tell me you think of your affair with Andoni as being in your childhood. We weren't just kids anymore then, but it's not bad as a distancing strategy."

"What did I write to you about childhood memories?" The cigarette smoke you blow out slowly, or maybe some sort of embarrassment, heats your cheeks, your right cheek especially. Why does one side blush more than the other?

"That we're at the time of life when childhood memories start to fade into the distance, or something like that."

You answer with a deep sigh and look down. "I wrote that to you?"

The attractive color of Andoni's skin about twenty years ago comes to your mind. When you were still too much of a child, when you still couldn't bring yourself to speak to him. Andoni. You don't know for sure when you started believing that he was the man for you. At least that's what you thought by the time you went to Italy together, that you were at the beginning of the life you would spend with him. In that hotel in Genoa, when you made love with him for the first time, when you made love for the first time. You wanted it to be a beginning, a beginning with him, a bond. You believed it. The first time your body shook the way it shook in that hotel in Genoa. You don't know if it ever happened so completely again.

"Did you go to see Andoni?" he asks, a smile in his voice, as if he hadn't heard your question.

"Yes, I didn't think twice about it. What else could I do? There wasn't any other way to talk directly to Andoni. You know he's lived in a house with no phone for the last couple of years and they told me he was home sick from work. I got scared, or worried anyway. Later, it wasn't such a big deal. To tell the truth, I don't know what I expected. I found him very thin and he didn't say much. He seemed beaten down. Like a lot of other people." You smile without lifting your gaze from the floor yet. "But he's more comfortable than a lot of other people, maybe that's the scariest thing, his calm. I thought that was probably what scared Jon."

"Did you see him?"

"Who, Jon?"

He nods.

"No, while I was there he didn't show up. I think he lives with his mother, with Andoni's wife. When he was little, I never saw him. I'm not going to start complicating things now. I didn't tell Andoni why I went to see him, and he didn't ask."

"He must have told his son to call."

Again a smile you don't see is in Luis' voice and, reaching out your right hand, you punch him lightly on the upper arm. The heat that rose in your cheeks before is now in your throat. The heat that rises from within. How you love this man. How you love Luis. You would cry if there were no space, time, context, tomorrows, yesterdays. If there were no yesterdays, on the other hand, you would not now be at Luis' side in his kitchen, in the present Luis' kitchen, at the past Luis' side.

Luis from the window of the bus, Luis with a young woman on Urbieta street, laughing. Many years ago, too many years ago to matter. No, it does matter. It matters because it mattered and, that day, seeing Luis laughing with that young woman on his arm made you withdraw from him. Distanced you. More than you thought at the time, for longer than you thought at the time. Or else it matters that it doesn't matter now, or what matters is to behave as if it didn't matter, to love as you love now, the inner happiness and pleasure that touching his arm gives you. What matters, matters. No more, no less.

You never told Luis. You never asked him who that woman was. A huge stupidity. Why ask? There must have been lots of women in Luis' life.

But you didn't see them.

You didn't see them on Urbieta street on a rainy Sunday afternoon, arm in arm and laughing, you on the bus on your way to have lunch at your parents' house without really feeling like it. They were both laughing. It looked like they were happy and you weren't happy, and you weren't a part of that happiness, you were inside the bus, watching through the window. Watching, but separate. The window, the dirty glass, the drops of rain on the dirty glass and the noise of the street on a Sunday afternoon on Urbieta street waiting for the traffic light to turn green.

You never said anything to him, but that year you didn't give Luis a birthday present. You called him to say happy birthday, but you didn't arrange to have coffee or go to the movies. Maybe you haven't called him to say happy birthday since. You know you sent him a postcard sometimes when his birthday happened to fall when you were traveling. But you haven't called. Traveling is its own excuse for sending a postcard. But if you call, the other person's voice is right there. They answer, they have to answer. They might question it. You haven't called him on his birthday for a long time. Certainly not since the day of Urbieta street.

Besides, then he went to W. and you got married. You didn't have much word of each other. Christmas cards from time to time. And you were very busy at work. Magazine work, articles and trips. Birthday or happy new year cards. Marriage. Family life. Family life times two, yours and Andrés', ever since things got serious between you. Had you already started seeing Andrés by the time of Urbieta street? That's not important, really.

You were with Andoni before, totally giddy with the attractiveness of this man twelve years older than you. Luis was always there. Luis was some other thing. He has always been some other thing. Something more internal or more external. Different. So different that you often forget it. He himself you'll never forget. It is what there is between the two of you that you remember only when something hurts you.

Maybe that was the last year you called him, the year you saw him on Urbieta street with that young woman. You didn't even arrange to go out for coffee. You didn't feel like going out with him.

Or?

He didn't make things easy himself either. You'd see each other some time, he said, or you said. You both said. And that's where things stood. You'd see each other some time.

Seems like this is it, that time has arrived.

Saturday, 5:15 pm

Luis makes an exaggerated show of falling in answer to your soft punch on his arm and smiles after you as you head for the door.

While he smiles at you, Luis is thinking he should call Elisabeth.

He promised he would call her, he would call her on the weekend. Tomorrow is still the weekend, but saying you'll call on the weekend doesn't mean you'll call on Sunday. In order to do something on the weekend, you have to meet on Saturday or Friday.

Luis knows Elisabeth will be waiting for his call, he knows she won't be left with nothing to do and even if he doesn't call she won't get mad, but he knows if he calls, she'll be very happy. Elizabeth's happiness, her overblown happiness, drowns him, he overflows with the weight of responsibility, but he's not capable of escaping. He would like to forget, like he has forgotten totally during these last few minutes talking to you, like he totally forgot about Elisabeth, about Elisabeth's powers of understanding, about Elisabeth's equilibrium, Elisabeth's quiet calm, Elisabeth's maturity, Elisabeth's particular individuality, forget about Elisabeth, forget about his obligation to Elisabeth.

"I should make a phone call," says Luis, without giving it much weight.

"About work?" You were on your way out of the kitchen. Your tone, too, is light.

"No, something else," and he stands up behind you, leaving the kitchen.

But maybe that call isn't about something else for Luis. When Elisabeth left him, arranging to meet her became like work. Before, when she lived with him, she was there, she came back after work to go out for dinner or to make a salad with him. Why did she leave? He said he understood, but it wasn't true, he didn't understand why she left, he didn't understand what was missing. And besides, he didn't know where she would find that missing thing, whatever it was. Would living alone give her what living with him for three years didn't provide?

If only she were angry, if she had gotten mad, if she had at least left screaming that it was all his fault, all Luis' fault.

But no, she left calmly, sad but calm.

Elisabeth was like that. Presumably she had thought a lot about it. She had turned it over and over in her mind, she told him when she came back tanned and beautiful after spending a few weeks alone in the Alps. There was no need to get angry, it would just be another stage in their lives. Another stage, another era, another cycle, another time. They could keep seeing each other, would keep seeing each other, he should call her, she'd call him too, they'd go to movies and things. If something else came of it, then good, maybe not going to bed together every day would respark their interest. That was the worst, having to call to be able to see her again, to be able to meet again. Why did she leave? Why did she go, what was she looking for?

Maybe she was making room for you.

Maybe, so that you could come with your husband, maybe Elisabeth left to make a little space in Luis' home, in Luis' life. When she had come, she too came in the same way, to fill a gap. Elisabeth decided to come and Elisabeth left because she wanted to leave, beautiful Elisabeth, Elisabeth's long blond hair and black dresses, her well-maintained body, strong, young.

In the evenings Luis feels Elisabeth's absence and the empty space she left in his nightly bed swells when he imagines her breasts in his hands.

The memory of Andoni's love
remains in your breasts as well.
Andoni's masculine hands,
like cups, sheltering your young breasts and
the heat of Andoni's chest close against
your back. The bitter taste of Andoni's
leaving remains in your throat.

The pain is still alive, sleeping in the
less pert breasts you have now, lurking in your
worn-out throat. From there you can call up
the images of that hotel room and the echoes of
Andoni's voice. And you do call them up,
like old wounds awakening to
feel the itch, because incomprehensible memories
have to be exposed again and again.

The first light of dawn had started to enter through the partings
of the hotel's heavy curtains. You had hardly
slept all night, but you weren't at all
sleepy.

Andoni's voice came to you from afar,
it seemed, even though his mouth
was closer to your ear, when he said you would
have to live without him, it would be better
without him, it was for your own good, you
were still very young and had lots to do in life,
your life had hardly begun, but his was
decided, his destiny marked out, he had
a son too and that would always
be a shackle, he didn't want to tie you down,
he loved you a lot, he'd had a wonderful time
with you (that much you knew, you know),
but take this trip as a goodbye.

You didn't answer him. You didn't defend yourself.
At that very moment you understood everything
as clear as day. You knew from the sound of
his voice there was no turning back,
he had already decided, that's how things would be,
if you said anything, it would only make things
worse.

You kept quiet, silent, so clearly did you
see the truth. His truth. You saw it
and felt the wound it made
in your flesh like a sword. You saw his truth
devouring yours. Your trembling, your surety,
your love, your happy thought that
he would be yours, your desire to have
his children… You saw your truths
torn to pieces, destroyed. Your ocean
of shining evening waves
was suddenly a dirty puddle on the edge of the highway,
a puddle emptied by the wheels of a truck. The gulls
no longer called, the sun didn't
turn the blue sea to gold.
As if the sharp sword of his truth had cut your vocal cords,
not even the sound of your breath escaped your throat
that freshly torn morning
in the hotel room in Genoa.

Winter
Negua
Invierno
Hiver
Winter
Hōtoke
Dzmer
Sharada
Dongtian
Fuyu

Friday, 11:40 pm

It's snowing outside. A candle on each of the small tables in the bar. It's comfortable. It must be almost midnight. Time for Friday to turn into Saturday. Miles Smiles, the name of the place. The music goes with the name. Miles Davis' music.

You're drinking wine, French wine, to overcome the inner and outer cold, to not feel foreign surrounded by a foreign language. The citizens of W. who go out at night don't seem foreign, don't seem that foreign in the warm atmosphere. Besides, the foreigners are you, really. Luis is also a foreigner, even though he has learned the language well. In some places it's not enough to study the language. Foreign. As foreign as Miles Davis. But Miles isn't a foreigner either in this place, at this hour. Sometimes language doesn't matter. But only sometimes.

How sad and how beautiful Miles Davis' trumpet seems to you. Miles Smiles. Miles doesn't smile. He died. He's dead. Miles. The San Sebastián Jazz Festival. A summer duty of youth. How many evenings you filled thanks to jazz and to the scandal of your elders. That's probably why you started liking jazz music, because your parents, your parents and their friends, didn't like the people that came to San Sebastián for the festival.

San Sebastián's tidy people.

San Sebastián's upright, boring citizens. A tidy, merry little city. You liked the Jazz Festival much better than the regattas. The native people from the province. On race days, Sundays, that folk music they played over the loudspeakers in Alderdi Eder park. They must have hung the loudspeakers from the tamarind trees. You never saw them. Or you forgot. Now, remembering the regattas pushes you deeper into melancholy than remembering the Jazz Festival. Your little summer dresses. The beginning of September, the first smell of the beginning of the end of summer. The days would be getting shorter, time to buy books for the new school year.

The three of you are drinking silently. At the same table. Each keeping to himself.

Luis looks at you. In the light of the candle your skin looks whiter or your lips darker. Like the color of wine.

Luis was waiting for you for a long time, even if he hadn't realized it until almost now.

He knew it would happen, whatever the obstacles, you would come. He never felt in any hurry, maybe that's why he didn't even realize what he already knew. Until now he had never felt in any hurry. But now, since you've

been together, the things he's forgotten are coming back
to life one by one.

Teresa's forgotten perfume.

How you empty a bit of tobacco from your cigarettes
before lighting them, turning them between your thumb
and forefinger.

A habit you picked up from him.

Before you came to W., for years, ever since that first
and last time, he has thought you would go to bed together again, more times, more often. Fantasies. Images of you
as lovers. He didn't know how, he wasn't in a hurry, he was
enjoying the not knowing or the laziness or the fear. Fear
of overanalyzing. Or the lack of will. Maybe.

Suddenly, with a telephone call, the lethargy ceased.
Luis' call broke his timeless gaze at you, his thoughts.
Until he made that call, you were a constant element of
his life. And would be in the future, he thought, for years.
It's also true that until the day of the call, especially since
you finished your studies and started working, sometimes
you didn't see each other for ages.

You didn't even have word of each other for years.

But you were there, somewhere, in some place he
didn't need to locate precisely, on his same wavelength.

On one of your birthdays, your twenty-eighth or so,
Luis called you on the phone. To say happy birthday. He
didn't call you every year, but he remembered every year.
When he called you that year, your cold answers ripped
him open from the throat down. A hole, a fracture, a
slash, a sting. Luis was ashamed of singing Happy
Birthday when he heard your dry thanks.

Then it was true.

You were getting married. You were someone else.
You were a Teresa getting married. A fiancée, a bride. You

weren't his Teresa, the Teresa of university holidays, Teresa who sang the songs of Paco Ibañez, Teresa who walked with him to the end of the pier commenting on the ways of the world. Lost Teresa who found her way. He had lost Teresa. Paths found, the certainty in another man must have given your voice that hardness. That voice that left him out.

It was true.

It was true, then, that you were getting married and it seemed impossible that it could cause him so much pain. He remembers that he felt like something had been taken from him. That calm, that limitlessness, the difficulty of defining the relationship between the two of you had ended. The comfort, the freedom, small or large, was over.

Luis gave up.

Right at that time, things were getting complicated and like the thunder after lightning, Luis suddenly got the opportunity to go abroad. Abroad, to finish his doctorate and teach in a place with good libraries, to live in a place where research was as important as teaching. Goodbye to his own little niche, goodbye for a while to no place like home, goodbye, goodbye to you too, goodbye to the gang and to going out in the rain to the old part of town.

He would leave.

He would go for a few years. Seeking oxygen. Going to forget you. To use a different language, just one, a single language for the whole day, a language that wasn't his. To read the newspapers with the detachment of distance… He would have to see for how long. He would know when to return from the way things went.

He left.

He left and he didn't come back. You, yes, you returned, you turned back toward him, came to him. You and your husband, this tall man at your side, this silent, handsome man, your offering, the gift you bring to the sacrificial altar. Things are good with you and Andrés, good people, made for each other, but made for him too. You, at least, are also his, always, and Luis always knew you were his, you were something of his, a friend, no other explanation required, intimate company, unconditional companionship even if you didn't see each other for years. He thought. Used to think. Thoughts. Dreams. Fantasies.

Friday, 11:45 pm

"*Voulez-vous danser avec moi?*" you say to Andrés, touching his shoulder with yours, elbows on the table, chin on fist. You're not drunk, but you're not far off. Enough not to feel the fatigue, to dare to say what you said to Andrés and to feel a heady urge to touch Luis. Andrés smiles at you and says that you know he doesn't know how to dance.

Then, still smiling, he says to Luis, with a funny tone in his voice, "Will you please dance with my wife?"

All is lost. Does Andrés know or doesn't he? Yes, he knows, he must know and he likes it. What does he know? How much does he like it? You don't care, you'd rather not think about it. Put yourself first for once. The alcohol helps you. The alcohol and the music. Miles Davis' trumpet plays *In Your Own Sweet Way*. It's cold outside. You can see snow through the window. It seems as if time has stopped.

You've been married for seven years. Long enough to have learned that even the smallest illusion dries up. That's illusion. A lie that looks like truth for a while. Nothing masked as something, a deception. All is lost.

You no longer have the dreams you had ten years ago and then you didn't have the dreams of ten years earlier either. The suspicions and fears of the time, yes. Fears aren't lost. Suspicions solidify.

You kept on living, impelled by something like inertia. At work. Especially at work. The inertia of work. Because of inertia. Or because you saw no other way. Or is it irrelevant in the end? There's nothing to do until death but live, and in the meantime, you have to spend your time doing something.

Even the love (do you remember how handsome Andoni was, when he started to sing on those earlier trips of yours?) that seemed to be the solution to all the boredom and misery you saw in people older than you turned into inertia. And there you are, forgetting the inertia of love by dint of work. In the inertia of love pushed by the inertia of work. In the inertia of love hidden by the inertia of work. A chain of inertia. The chain that binds you.

Lord, set us free.

Set us free and give us, give us this day our daily bread. Food and drink. Alcohol. A thousand faces of a single thing. Impossible to think any more. Your insides melt and the only real thing is Luis' arm, Luis' arm around your waist. You feel yourself loving Luis, not like before (how did you love him before?), but you love him. Not like when you used to walk to the end of the pier together, but you want to keep dancing with him. Oh, if only the music would never stop! You would go on a trip with him. Or go to bed. Go to bed and make love until dawn and wake up slowly the next day and draw pictures on his chest with your fingers as if there were no such thing as time, without speaking. You prefer not to speak. You don't want to break the distance of so many years. Silence. You weren't all that close before either. What did Luis think? Now at least he's not saying anything and, holding you by the waist, he pulls you close in a soft hug.

Why does death never arrive at such times?

You and Luis dancing. A bit run-down, but attractive, an attractive couple. What ties you together now, still, you and Luis? What purpose do memories, good memories, serve, how far will they take you? Yes, say what you like, you have good memories of what you shared with Luis, whatever it was. What was it? You told Andrés that you and Luis had gone to bed together once, like a kind of ritual between friends, to pay some sort of debt, to do what the modern kids of the time had to do.

Andrés is sure that Luis likes you.

Andrés always thinks that other men must like his wife. You're attractive. You look good, way better than average. Many other men must like you.

That's what Andrés thinks.

Besides, you know how to exploit your charm. Andrés likes that other men like you, he shows you off. He urges you to buy new clothes. Lately it seems that if he didn't encourage you, you wouldn't buy anything. Only decorations for the house, as if you wanted to make your surroundings pretty: your surroundings but not yourself. Andrés likes you to wear pretty clothes, to change, to show off the slenderness of your body. Through the glances of other men, Andrés pays you nightly with the passion which has long since grown weak for you.

Maybe because of that, because he won't look at you directly, he hardly notices, or only from time to time does he perceive how your slenderness is becoming frailty, how you wear only loose clothing, looser and looser, your clothes fall off you more and more.

Andrés finds it arousing to watch you dancing with Luis. Exciting. A drunken voyeur. He imagines the two of you fucking in the hazy images of his pickled brain. A big bed and purple sheets is what he sees.

Friday, 11:50 pm

When the song ends, you go to the bathroom. After peeing, you wash your hands. Why shouldn't you wash them before peeing? The contagion that your piss can spread to the world is apparently more dangerous than that that can be carried from the world to your insides on the thin paper in your hands. The world is clean, piss is dirty. Your piss. You are dirty. You step on the pedal that opens the lid of the trash can. The traces of some other woman's blood on a sanitary napkin in the trash. Someone else's, not yours, it isn't yours.

For a long time you haven't left any traces of blood, any traces of female menstrual blood. It must be maybe two months without a period, yes, more than two months, a lot more than two months (how could it not be more than two months!). You've been here for three months, you came here three months ago, just about exactly three months ago now, on the last day of November, and you haven't had to buy any sanitary napkins yet.

For the last couple of years it's been like that. You've had recesses, droughts. Maybe not so long. The doctor told you not to worry.

Women's menstrual blood.

One chance to get pregnant every month, twelve chances every year, twelve times I-don't-know-how-many.

Times twenty. No, more. You got your first period before you were fifteen. Thirteen. Twelve times twenty-two chances, twelve times twenty-two refusals. You feel something nipping at your back. Maybe God is punishing you for refusing so many times and now you can't.

Bear a child. *Haurdun*. Child-bearing. What an expression. What a backward language. Too many priests inventing the vocabulary. Too many doctrines creating tradition.

Before you came here, when was your last period, your monthlies, that monthly worry. You don't know. Before, earlier, you always wrote it down. You always marked at least the first day in your calendar. Before, earlier, when you didn't want to get pregnant, when you used to risk getting pregnant. The fears, pleasures and risks of lost virginity, the fear of passion, the enjoyment of risk.

The shine of alcohol in your eyes in the image of your face in the mirror over the sink. Tears also make eyes shine, but you haven't cried for a long time. You haven't marked down the first day of your period for a long time either, unless it's time for your yearly visit to the gynecologist, since that's the first thing the gynecologist asks you on your yearly visit, when was your last period. The question about your period repeated every year. Why do they ask so often, if it doesn't matter in the end? When was your last period? The yearly question about your monthlies. When was the last one? No, don't worry, it's probably just nerves. The big table and gentle smile of the gynecologist. It's still early to think about menopause, but sometimes, not very often... Your gynecologist writes with a fountain pen. How old are you? When was your last one, when will the next one be, when will the next one be, will there be a next one, will there ever be a next one, another one? When, Teresa, was your last period, the dark trace of your period, that dark red of red wine?

Andrés has ordered more wine. He doesn't want to think about tomorrow. He has packed his suitcase and prepared his papers. The trip isn't too long. The time of departure, comfortable. The work he has to do isn't too hard either. Boring. He knows he'll be bored in the end-less self-important meeting. How to help the third world. How to help the third world without giving anything up ourselves, without losing anything of ours, earning the goodwill of the companies on whom the unity of nations depends, making them rich, how to sell our help, how to display our goodness in the newspapers.

The wine is really good. Or no, maybe it's not that good, but he's drunk enough by now.

Tomorrow he'll go on the plane. The careful hands of the stewardesses. The careful, professional smiles of the stewardesses. The careful hands of the stewardesses are no fantasy. Another level of image. The images of tomorrow, of a real tomorrow, the ones that will certainly happen. He'll go tomorrow.

Space and time: tomorrow, go, him.

He fills his glass with wine. So what. Better not to think. Why worry. Things are what they are. He'll return. Life will go on. You'll be waiting. You never go away. You have no need to. It's enough for you to sink into your own thoughts. The shelter of silence. Your resources. Luis is a nice boy. You're friends and that's good. Who would ever have thought Andrés would be happy to listen to Miles Davis? Those are the surprises life offers. Everything else is known.

Saturday, 3:15 pm

An hour ago you said goodbye to Andrés at the passport control desk in the airport. Passports and borders, they say there are no borders in Europe any more. He took out his passport after giving you a kiss, but they didn't even look at it. You think the policeman smiled at him. He had kept the guy ahead of Andrés at the window for a long time. His skin was darker than Andrés' and his clothes were a lot cheaper, a lot older.

On the way back from the airport, you stop and look around the Christmas market. How long Christmas lasts here, Christmas decorations, songs, markets. You're not in a hurry to get home. You'd like to, but there's no rush. There aren't many people in the market stalls, just a few, looking around like you. Looking without buying. The buyers must be at home making Saturday dinner, arguing with their kids, amusing themselves with television programs or who knows what. Whoever hasn't got a home to spend Saturday afternoon in is out on the streets in the cold. The poor. Here too there are poor people, people of color, dark, darker than you at least, like the guy they stopped at passport control in the airport. His brothers and sisters. His or somebody else's, someone's brothers and sisters, some mother's sons and daughters. Migrants, immigrants, the poor from somewhere. Broken shells, homes left behind somewhere, shattered snails. The rest must be snug and cozy in the homey warmth of a long afternoon. At home. In the afternoon warmth.

Saturday, 4:30 pm

Once you get home, you try to work. You're seated in front of the computer. Thinking about the poor dark-skinned people in the Christmas market and at the metro stop. Wanting to empty your mind. Wanting to forget about writing. Making an effort at the legitimate escape of writing. Not a single sentence. You want to get those darker, poorer, uglier people out of your head. You also don't want to think about Luis, who had to go to the university right after breakfast. You especially don't want to remember Luis. Who knows why he went? Better, anyway, that he not be home now. A significant action for him. Did he do it deliberately? No, probably not. He said he needed some notes from his office to prepare some article or other. It's better now that he's not home yet. A break after saying goodbye to Andrés, a break without Andrés or Luis. Time out. *Tiempo muerto*. Dead time, silent time.

But there's no silence, no emptiness inside you. Andrés' goodbye and the dark-skinned people's clothes and Luis' absence and the clatter of last night's wine and tobacco shoo away your ability to come up with sentences.

Suddenly, steps on the stairs? Yes, footsteps. Your heart races and the rhythm of your breath changes. One sentence, you try to write just one sentence. You look at the blue computer screen, trying not to hear the sound of keys in the lock. *The color of the poor.* Instead of these words you had in mind, you write *Darkness* on the screen, as if your fingertips went faster than your thoughts. You feel the weight of last night's wine in the middle of your forehead. There's no more room for sadness in your body.

You won't go to Luis, even though you hear him stop in the entrance hall. Stationary for ten seconds or so, then footsteps coming toward your room. You're afraid, you know, you want, but thinking about what you want scares you too, naming what you want, giving it a precise form. Could Luis want it too? Could you be ruining something? Both of you? Just you. Where are you going, toward what?

Maybe you're imagining everything. Andrés will also return, he'll be back in a couple days. Did Andrés know? Yes, he knew, some sort of thankfulness that you recognize and hate is inside you, rising between your belly and your breasts.

Luis is coming into your room. You don't move from the computer. You don't even look behind you, toward the door. Your hands are motionless in your lap, as if resting, impotent. Luis has reached you and he hugs you, bending over, from behind, his face sinking into the nape of your neck, lips quickly brushing your skin. His breath gives you shivers.

"Don't say anything, Luis." Despair is in your eyes, but you can't see your own eyes. You feel the bittersweet-ness of your voice in your throat. Then you add in a soft-er voice, "I'd rather you didn't say anything." You don't want to turn, you don't want to see Luis, you close your eyes.

Straightening up, Luis takes your head in his hands and pulls you gently toward him. You lift your face and Luis bends again until his lips reach yours. The tremor that runs from your lips all the way down your back takes your breath away.

You'll drown. You want to stand, you'll explode if you don't hug him, if you aren't touching from head to toe. The unstoppable kiss that drives you crazy. How long have your bodies been waiting for this moment? You're about to faint and you look to Luis for help and you see in his smile that he's happy, very happy, as happy as you are and you believe you're friends. You want to believe it with all your heart. To believe it, to believe it again.

You don't say anything, either of you. Luis takes you by the hand and leads you to his room. He closes the door in the middle of the hall in passing. He takes you to his side of the house.

Sunday, 8:03 am

The room is full of the new light of morning. The high white walls reflect the feeble winter sun. Luis feels your cheek, your ear and your hair against his chest. He knows you're waking up, but he doesn't look at you, he prefers to keep his eyes shut, feeling how you move your head a little bit and how you give him a light kiss. Shivers. Then he moves his hand from between your shoulders to your ass, drawing a straight line down your back, gentle, with the tip of his middle finger. You get goosebumps all over.

You snort in a faint laugh, but you don't say anything, you don't dare, you don't want to look up, you don't want to see Luis' face yet. The bare walls of the room are painted white. The ceiling is very high. The curtains are white too. The stucco design around the edges of the ceiling is very pretty, plump roses. You look into the mirror at the side of the bed and, lifting your face a bit, you see yourself in the mirror, you and Luis between the white sheets. Luis smiles at you from the mirror. You like the image in the mirror. *The image in the mirror…* you think. The sentence tails off on its own, it's as if it had come from somewhere else. You should write it down.

If there were no time, if there were no world, but especially, if there were no time. The dizziness of last night comes to you like music from afar. Your throat tightens, you could almost cry and you hold tight to Luis' muscular chest. You move your bodies in parallel and tremble in the exchange of your dried blended sweat. Your fatigue has turned into gales of laughter and Luis says he could eat up your laughter. He wraps you in his hug, lies on top of you, his lips one with yours, you feel his penis against your belly, hot and full. He starts moving up and down. You raise your hips toward him, toward his sex, squeezing his penis with your desire.

You're melting, eyes closed, gathering force, holding and releasing your breath, finally exploding, you're a volcano, a September wave against the Paseo Nuevo, the center of the giant gong the orange-clad Buddhist priests strike, an explosion, the fastest of Niagara's falls, August fireworks on the beach. You love Luis, you want to swallow him whole or disappear inside him, you disappearing in his heat, melting in his wetness, let the flow of his sperm spread over you.

Perfection, a flawless moment, total happiness, absolute present.

Sunday, 8:53 am

Everything is calm again in the mirror, the sheets, Luis' arm, your hair.

> There lay Al-Ith, rocked on the man's strong breast, all cradled and comforted, sobbing away, just as she had wanted to do on so many occasions recently. That she didn't believe in the efficacy of it did not prevent her enjoying it, while it lasted.
> DORIS LESSING,
> *The Marriages between Zones Three, Four, and Five*

Did not prevent her... while it lasted. While it lasted. As long as it lasts, enjoy.

Sunday, 9:45 am

Luis stays in bed when you rise to shower. Arms over his head, hands beneath. He seems to be looking at the ceiling.

You feel lost.

On your way to the bathroom, Luis admires your ass. You're older than Elisabeth, that's what he thinks. Your ass is also older than Elisabeth's, but he can still tell that you've done quite a lot of exercise. Luis has liked your ass for a long time. An image of the two of you running on the beach flashes through Luis' mind. You must be thirty-five, he calculates. Yes, the two of you were the same age. Or within a year one way or the other. He remembers you finished your degrees the same year anyway.

You go into the bathroom and, seeing that you need to put on a new toilet roll, you give thanks for the peace that comes from knowing what to do for a moment.

You've always had the habit of imagining movies to yourself when you hear music, you don't know when you started doing it. It seems to you that you've always done it, ever since you grew into yourself. An escape or a consolation, who cares. Often you fill the scripts with different characters, but there's one that always has Luis as the main character. Certain songs by Bruce Springsteen or Hertzainak bring it to mind: you're walking past a bar in Donostia and you see that Luis is inside, Luis sees you too and stops to stare at you until you enter. Inside, you start to dance together. Today you don't know what to do with your fantasies. You'd like to shut down your imagination.

Memory, recollection, that's life, the only way of life, the space one person may have in another. Does love not mean giving someone else a good place in your memory, a tender place, leaving a space for them? What else could love be? Luis will have that tender space inside you. He has it. He has always had it. Andrés too. Forever. Since the beginning. Because you wanted it that way. You get in the

shower. Cold. The first spray is always cold even if the
water is scorching. That's exactly what it's like. You see
your skin red as a lobster. To burn, to clean yourself with
hot water, totally. You scrub one arm hard, the left, your
legs, knees and thighs, the fine hair between your legs,
your belly. You used a condom last night. Good, very
good. Luis didn't stop you. Nor in the morning. He did-
n't penetrate you, but he satisfied himself. Do men need
to satisfy themselves? And women? You? Last night you
didn't have an orgasm, but you felt fantastic. That may be
satisfaction.

The sweet pain around your clitoris brings back the
recent rubbing repeated again and again. To your memory and to your skin. It doesn't seem to have gotten any
worse than last night. It might be true anyway that if men
don't enter you with their penis they're left with unending
frustration. The myth of penetration. The dogma against
penetration. More myths. How much wasted time. Too
much. How much time, how many interminable debates.
But now, history's revenge. Men, women, males and
females without reaching an agreement, still with so much
yet to understand between them, the fear of disease. What
Emma Thompson said in an interview comes back to you.
Her generation, your generation, was the last to have sex
without fear. The last and the first, you added when you
read that. Without fear and deliberately, in the hope that
the world would become a better place that way, and your
world was better, freer. Bravo to those who prefer the
cleanliness of virginity, those who equate sex with moth-
erhood, those who believe in one true love. Nature has
been cruel with the rest, with ones like you. Maybe it was
always like that, but when you were young, when the
echoes of the hippies reached you, when you started

smoking joints, when you learned to buy pills to avoid getting pregnant, it didn't seem Nature could ever be cruel to anyone who didn't fear it. It's true that Nature is cruel or God exists and that this cruel God seems to have won over Nature.

Fear of disease. The threat of punishment. The time spent in debate was wasted. Worthless.

No, Luis didn't object. Why should he? He must be used to it. He must be used to it with Elisabeth. Elisabeth. Where is Elisabeth? Does Elisabeth love Luis? Elisabeth's health. Take care of Elisabeth's health.

You want to know what's wrong with you. What's happening to you. Why you haven't had a period for months. Why you're always so tired. No, you don't want to know because you don't want to be sick, you don't want to have anything, you want to live. It's just nerves. That's what they told you before anyway. Stress, fatigue. You should go for analysis.

You don't want to know. You don't want to be sick. Or do you? Do you hope your body will speak at last, will force you to do something, will drive you to ask something of somebody? Help. Perhaps help is the love you don't know how to ask for.

Sunday, 10:00 am

"How's Elisabeth?" you yell without leaving the bathroom.

Luis didn't expect any questions at all. Especially not that one.

"Are you asking if I'm still with her?" he asks you with what might pass for a yawn.

"Yes and no." Your voice is almost challenging.

AND THE SERPENT SAID TO THE WOMAN 63

"I haven't seen her lately, I think she's abroad. She had some kind of opening ceremony." It sounds like he has sat up on the bed. His voice no longer sounds like he's lying down.

It makes Luis angry not to remember more clearly and he's tempted to lie. He doesn't want to appear defenseless before you. He doesn't want you to think that you are now his only dream, that he's obsessed with you. Or does he want you to guess that? That or something very like it. Anyway, he would prefer that his relationship with Elisabeth seem to you to be closer than it is. He thinks that way you'll fight to win him. His initial spontaneity is turning into anger. Why did you have to come out with Elisabeth just now?

"You're not together." The tone of victory.
"To tell the truth, I don't know about together, when were we ever together?" Luis answers without having time to make up something else.

Without the time or the inclination to make up something else. Who knows? Maybe it's better to tell the truth. The truth as he understands it. Does he understand it? What does he care now? Now all he cares about is how to extricate himself from your web of questions.

"Well, whatever." The beginning of anger might be in your voice.

Luis grasps a small hope. Maybe you're joking or half-joking. Luis would rather you came out of the bathroom so he could see you.

"No, it's true," he says softly.

Luis would like to get out of this conversation. How did it start? Why are you talking about him and Elisabeth?

"It's unbelievable what you men are like." You've lost control of your thoughts, words escape you on their own. You go into the bedroom drying your hair on the white hand towel. You hang your head upside down, hair swinging. You don't want to look at Luis.

Luis can't see your face.

"Really. Doesn't anything ever last inside you? What does it mean to you to be with someone? What's the point of having a thing with someone, going to bed with them, fucking?" The words fly out faster and faster, something is hurting you a lot.

When you straighten up, your face is bright red, as if your upside-down anger has almost strangled you. Luis almost laughs, but when your sad expression strikes him, his smile freezes half-way.

"Hey, take it easy! You're not going to hit me with a big feminist speech now, are you?" Luis tries to sound like he's joking, he doesn't know if it will work.

Standing at the foot of the bed, you look at Luis lying down. You narrow your eyes to say, "I don't know. Maybe it would have been better if we hadn't gone to bed. That way you would always have wanted to and that would have been some sort of bond with me."

When you look at him from the foot of the bed, it seems to Luis that you're very far away from him. Hoping to regain the peace, he says, "That's a pretty flimsy bond, isn't it? It's better like this. Going to bed strengthens the bond. I don't see why if there's a good thing between two people, if they're friends and there's an attraction, they can't go to bed together. That's the most natural thing, isn't it? We're making it all too cosmic, I think."

The same old story, heard
over and over. A piece of friendship.
Just as well, if there's at least a piece. But
for that you need friendship. For something
to be a piece of another something, you need
the whole, and do men have that? Do they?
Why do they forget, then, everything,
totally. Why doesn't Luis care in the least
where Elisabeth is, what she's doing, if she's well
or sick. How can that not have any
presence in Luis' mind, in his heart,
in his gut… Maybe it's not true they don't care
at all. Maybe something at least matters to them
sometimes, but they don't know what to do with the worry,
the unanswered questions, and they pretend to ignore it.
They ignore it so well, so long, so
systematically, that they erase
from memory that question, that source of worry,
like when an actor identifies so much with a role
that another's identity takes root,
like a writer who confuses himself
with his favorite character.

*Elastic: Said of what can be stretched or
deformed and, when the force that produces the stretching
or deformation is removed, recovers its original form.*

Men's love is elastic. You leave
no trace. Going to bed with men.
Making love. Thinking you touch
a man's soul. A rotten thought. The smell of corruption,
the stench, the filth. Adam's soul. Eve's
punishment. Allegedly touching. Letting it be touched.
Opening. Open your legs. Open your thighs. Open
your insides. Let him in. Let him become erect. Let him out,
to come back into you. Let them be one, your insides
with his outsides. A man's roar, a man's
tears, a man's soul. A union of souls.
An alleged omission, a rotten thought. Paper dream
of dreamless nights. Wanting and unable.
And the fatigue, the eternal fatigue, that
eternal fatigue of yours. That fatiguing fatigue you didn't have before
but that now seems eternal, an endless
unpardonable fatigue. An incessant fatigue,
endless fatigue, infinite fatigue.

Spring
Udaberria
Primavera
Primadera
Printemps
Frühling
Garun
Kōanga
Vasanta
Chuntian
Haru

Friday, 7:00 pm

The night before Saturday, Friday evening and still light. The colors and smells of spring. Luis isn't at home, he had to go back to his office to look for some papers he'd forgotten. Better. Better if Andrés weren't home either, you need to be alone, but on the other hand you're completely lazy. Yes, you'll get your jacket and go out. You'll buy the newspaper, you'll go to the metro stop where they sell the international edition of *El País*. On foot. Three quarters of an hour, yes, without stopping to look at too many shop windows. That way you'll get yourself moving a little bit. Maybe it will rain. You'd better take an umbrella; you should also buy some stockings, black. Your legs look longer and thinner in black stock-

ings. Even thinner. You feel like wearing a skirt and stockings, will you eat dinner out? Will Luis come, will he
come alone?

The sound of the telephone. The phone rings, rings
for you. You go to answer it slowly. It's Elisabeth.
Elisabeth, asking for Luis. You tell her he isn't home and,
unwillingly, add that he has gone to his office; if she calls
immediately she'll catch him there. She thanks you.
Thanks a lot. You're welcome, *bitte*, please. Soon after,
when Luis calls to say he won't be back for dinner, you
notice how light and happy his voice is. Wanting to make
it sound like a joke, you remark that you knew he had better plans. No, you weren't being nasty and you really do
hope he has a nice time. With all your heart, really. Bye,
goodbye Luis.

There are some old magazines on a shelf by the
phone, those old magazines. Why does Luis still have
them? He must have brought them. Maybe he has them
sent. A past issue of *Viejo Topo*, a few copies of *Ere*. When
did Luis go away? Maybe he was still a subscriber when he
came. When were those magazines shut down forever?
OK, *Viejo Topo* is being published again. Not *Ere*. *Ere* is
gone forever. *Ere* is also gone forever, like so many things
of the Basque Country, like so many ideas. You pick up a
copy of *Ere*. You can't remember what year the last issue
was published. You also don't know exactly how long it
survived, not long, a few short years. With a certain mor-
bid curiosity, maybe to hurt yourself, you open the magazine. What a coincidence, an interview with Marisa.
Curly hair, a black sweater and cigarette smoke. The
Marisa of the time.

> ...I think, anyway, that women are much more interesting than men,
> in general, and I know that these generalizations are hateful and often

stupid. I mean to say that the combination of calm adult person and child that women maintain is much more subtle than in men. Men do it in a much more shameless way, their fields of action are much more differentiated and more transparent at the same time. I don't know. I'm convinced that many women will understand exactly what I'm talking about.

At the time you wanted to be like Marisa, like her but prettier and calmer. At the time, you didn't really understand what she said, even though you thought she was right. What have you learned these last fifteen years, to realize that you understood things literally then, you translated them directly with your own interior dictionary.

Now what Marisa said then soaks you, like the waves at high tide that come in too fast. Unexpectedly. Suddenly. Cold.

But now, when you need them most, Marisa apparently doesn't say such things any more. Maybe now you understand the world less than ever and that's why you need those old slogans so much. In the time from then to now, your strength to despise Marisa's stories has slipped through the cracks. You find yourself weaker than ever, but nevertheless you realize almost with sadness the truth of Marisa's dark comments, the truth you don't understand, the senseless truth. You almost feel sadness, but there's no tragedy. Blind bitter fatigue. Nothing but blind bitter fatigue. The old Marisa's newly arisen fatigue, the fatigue that wound up turning into silence. Age.

Age, you thought then too, translated as a countable concept, *years* or *time*, in your interior dictionary. The age you are now is fatigue, a fall, a submersion into silence, closing your eyes like someone lying on the couch huddling under a blanket.

Then age meant wrinkles, six at the corners of each of Marisa's eyes. Those dark lines at the edge of Marisa's mouth, your young face, your plump skin. That was age. Something to count. You remember the sympathy that Marisa's male friends showed you, and Marisa's fruitless smile, her sad ironic gaze. You thought you were as bright as Marisa and prettier and that's why the men, the men of Marisa's age, preferred your young company. Marisa knew a lot. She knew a lot and she was beautiful, the beauty of this experienced forty-something woman and her svelte body come to your mind, and that thing about her hands.

Marisa used to say that he who fell in love with the motion of a hand was lost forever, there is no reasoning that might protect him, he will always love the owner of those hands, even if they bring him the greatest pain. At the time, when you were too young, you smiled. Now you think of Luis.

Friday, 7:05 pm

The sound of the telephone startles Luis. The halls of his building are empty, and there's no sound of anybody from the neighboring offices either. They sent him an article he had been looking for for a long time. As interesting as its title made it seem.

He couldn't stop reading it.

He doesn't even know how much time has passed since he got to his office. When the telephone rings, he looks at his watch as he stretches his arm out to pick up the receiver.

"Yes," he says without enthusiasm, still looking at his article.

"Is that any way to answer the phone? To tell the truth, I'm not surprised you're so glum, shut in there on a Friday evening. You'll turn into a book one of these days."

"Oh, Elisabeth. How are you? You startled me."

"You didn't expect me to call, huh? Do you remember me? That woman who used to live with you?"

"As if I'd forget!"

Later, Luis called home. He called you, to say he wouldn't be going out to eat, he wouldn't be coming back.

Why did he call you?

He notices a strange coldness in your voice, or sadness more than coldness, something like that. He doesn't like it. Why did he call you, can he not do as he likes in his own home, can he not come and go as he pleases, why does he have to account to you for his actions? On the other hand, it's normal to call. Lately you've been spending a lot of weekend afternoons together, most of them. Or does he want to check your response to him telling you he's going out with another woman? He remembers the time he called to tell you happy birthday, that last push he needed to decide to move abroad, the cold distance in the tone of your voice.

Saturday, 8:00 am

You wake up early, too early for a Saturday, but since you're not working, all days are alike. Saturday morning is different only if you go out Friday night. Sundays, because of the silence on the streets. Today is a gentle Saturday, you didn't go out yesterday.

Luis didn't come home. Normally you hear the sound of his key. But just in case, when you cross the border of the two apartments to go to the kitchen, you don't stop at

the kitchen, you pass the kitchen door and go to Luis'
bedroom. The door is ajar and you see his empty bed.

Without making any noise, on the tips of your toes
and without moving the door, almost without taking a
breath, as if someone were asleep in the bed and as nervous as if you were doing something secret, you enter Luis'
bedroom. You know he has a photograph of Elisabeth on
the wall by the bed. From the summer. She's smiling. The
look of someone loved or at least admired in her eyes, on
her lips. She has a wide mouth and her eyes… her eyes are
too far apart. You disgust yourself and force yourself to
admit that she's pretty, Elisabeth is a beautiful woman.
You keep looking at the photograph, standing, hands in
the pockets of your pink bathrobe. She has very beautiful
lips. Fleshy. How much more interesting women are to
you than men. How much more attractive. How much
greater, somehow, the curiosity they arouse in you.
Curiosity, envy, interest, admiration, but always more.
Something more.

Women are you.

Back to your room.

You don't go into the kitchen now either. You don't
want to start making breakfast. Beyond the kitchen, you
tread more calmly on the old wood of the floor, not afraid
to make noise. The wood needs waxing. You hear Andrés
in the shower. The bathroom door is ajar, the mirror is
steamed up. When you enter, the damp warmth sur-
rounds you.

"Con permiso?" you call in a Mexican accent, trying
for a playfulness you don't feel. You disgust yourself.
You're embarrassed.

"Come on in!" Andrés, strong, from behind the shower curtain. "I thought you left. I thought maybe you went jogging."

"Yes, I'm just about to."

"So?"

"I don't know, well, never mind, it doesn't matter."

"Yes, it does matter. Teresa, I don't know what's happening with you, but something's going on." Andrés' voice is softer than before, but gives away that he's losing patience.

"Yes, something's always going on," you say with a touch of arrogance. Then you continue, more softly, "I don't know, I don't know, I think I expected too much. I thought everything would be OK when we went abroad. But, to tell the truth, I don't know exactly what it was that needed to be fixed. Maybe things are just like that. The best thing would be not to give it too much importance."

"But you do, or at least you keep thinking about it…" He gets out of the shower and starts to dry off.

He looks tall, muscular, well-formed to you. As always. Your husband has always looked so solid to you.

You feel no desire at all to touch him. But you're also incapable of asking for help. Help with what?

"Because I have too much time on my hands. If only I could concentrate on work. I haven't written anything lately."

"You know what?" The quality of his voice has changed. He seems to want to sound cheerful. He sounds like he's talking to a child. "Tonight we'll go out for dinner, the two of us. Like we were dating. OK? That way Saturday will seem like a Saturday."

"If we're going to do that, we'll have to make a date. A rendezvous, by the cathedral, for example." For a second, your fatigue lightens. You're afraid to discuss your fear of illness. You mention your fatigue less and less. You haven't mentioned your period for the last few months. You need secrets. The perverse idea of keeping your misery to yourself.

Because you want to play Andrés' game, you feel a softness inside you. The magic of good will. Good will and faith.

They say faith can move mountains.

Saturday, 9:00 am

Andrés is on his way to the office. After two stops, the metro seems to turn into a tram. The metro comes out from under ground. The water one can see on both sides from the windows isn't frozen; for a long time there have been no ice-skaters on it. It's spring. But nobody is swimming yet either. The small sailboats are in drydock too. The houses are smaller now and farther apart. The area is looking less and less like a city. The European headquarters of the UN is on the outskirts of the city, it's not in town.

Andrés hadn't thought about it before today.

The city is left behind.

You are also left behind. He, Andrés, is going away on the metro. But he shouldn't think about you. He shouldn't waste his energy. He has to concentrate on work.

Next week he has to finish a report. He can't see the end of it. They must repair the seemingly irreparable. Nothing new will come of Monday's meeting. He has to think of something, he has to come up with something. Something that will make them believe the irreparable can be repaired. He'll come up with something. He has often been able to. That's why he was offered this contract. They know he's good and he has to remember that. Calm down. Gather his wits. Tease apart the problems, take them one by one and solve each one in its turn.

You used to say that. You, Teresa. You're a problem now, but no, you can't be Andrés' problem right now. He has to get you out of his head for a couple hours. When he leaves his office, he'll start thinking about you again. Luis thinks you're suffering, slowly. Luis thinks you're drying up. Slowly, endlessly drying up and suffering, without asking for help. Andrés realizes your sadness wears him out, your sadness, or not knowing what to do about your sadness. When he doesn't know what to do at work, it's just another bit of ignorance, bad but bearable. But in your case he can hardly stand it. Going to work, being away from you, should give him a little peace, the calm he needs to think.

He won't hear your quiet movements.

Andrés realizes that he's angry and he doesn't want to be angry. He doesn't want to be angry with his wife, with you. It doesn't seem right to him. It frightens him. The anger must be because of his helplessness, but he feels the anger toward you. Against you. You don't tell him what's going on with you, how he can help you, if you need something.

And he doesn't have time to start guessing.

He has to concentrate on work. He'll have to put in a lot of hours this coming week. He has to prove himself to the people who think he's good.

When Andrés went to his office (to his office or looking for someone from his office or whatever), when you were left alone at home, that frightening eternal emptiness rose inside you and paralyzed you. That first frightening silence from the beginning. Often, when there's no one home, the emptiness keeps you from getting out of bed. You put on music. Then you tidy up the plants and make tea. And you start to read.

Saturday, 9:30 am
    Andrés has reached his office. He hasn't managed to shake off your image. Where does your crazy melancholy come from? Maybe if you hadn't put aside the issue of children so easily. Maybe it's not too late. But no, this isn't the best time to talk to you about that. Something tells Andrés that much. Besides, does he want kids? If you had kids, you definitely wouldn't be where you are now, like you are now, as good as you are now, as bad as you are now.
    On the other hand, if your sadness isn't cured by children (if motherhood doesn't cure your sadness), what would a depressed mother pass on to her baby (what would you pass on to your and Andrés' baby)?
    You've never shown any envy when you've been with friends' kids. Once you said to Andrés that they bored you, not the children themselves, but conversations about parents and kids. When there were kids around, all the adults talked about kids or to kids and there was no way to have a decent conversation about anything interesting. Yes, that's what you told him. That or something like that. Andrés remembers. He remembers it well. He doesn't know exactly where it took place, but you weren't alone. You were with friends. At a dinner or something.
    It makes him feel like he's suffocating to imagine ordinary family life in his own home. The two of you have always been in complete agreement on this. You've never talked too much about it, it's true. Because there was no need to. That's why, because you were always in agree-

ment and there was no need for debate. That's the way it was. That's probably the way it was. That's what he thought, at least. You never said anything to deny it either. You're not one to remain silent. Or are you? You're often silent. Silent for a long time.

Who knows? Who knows what you're like? What do you think about ordinary family life now? Does he know what you're like, you, Teresa, what you're like now? Did he know what you were like when he married you?

You, at least, didn't know much about him. That's what Andrés thinks.

You told yourselves over and over that you understood each other very well. Often. Frequently. You believed it too and felt it. One person feels like he knows another when he falls in love, when he feels the desire to be with another. Luis, at least, didn't know everything about your life and there were many things you didn't know about Luis either.

That must be what getting to know someone is all about, learning the other person's stories, what happened to them, what they answered when somebody said such and such to them, what kind of dress you wore for your first communion and what kind of pencil sharpener your grandfather gave you for your first day of school. One's own biography. The other person's biography.

If that's knowing someone, Andrés knows you better now than before.

But he hasn't registered your recent changes. In learning your history, he lost the knowledge of you yourself, the present Teresa. Contact. You withdrew from him or he from you. You can see the distance.

Work. Damned work.

He likes work so much, his work. He enjoys devising projects, reaching agreements, selling ideas, meeting people from other places. Work. The work that leaves him without energy to be with you. Without the capacity to understand you. He doesn't get tired at work. He doesn't get tired the way he gets tired of your fatigue, the way he gets tired of fighting at home, the way he gets lost in the silence at home.

Saturday, 7:00 pm
     Once Andrés is gone and you start reading, the day picks up speed. You have to give time a push at first, so you don't drown under its weight. Then, from a certain moment on, time slides along on its own. To light candles, for that you interrupt your reading. And to eat something, some crackers. A little later, a sandwich. Cheese. And to answer the phone. Rarely.
     It rings a couple times. Once, a wrong number. The other, a message for Luis, a phone number; please call on Monday. Time goes faster as it passes, you notice it less and less. It slows down only when you think about Luis. When you think about Luis, time stops, like your breath, for a few seconds. He could call, couldn't he? At least to say he wasn't coming home. God, what are you thinking, why should he have to call, why should he have to call you? He's a big boy now and you're not his mother, you're not his anything.
     A friend of his.
     It's nice to be a friend, just a friend. What does it mean to be just a friend?
     Just.
     What else might there be? Platonic friendship, just friends, friendship with no touching, friendship with no

zing. What do you want, a bond, control? You have no right, you have no right at all, nobody has the right to control anybody else's life, but you especially have no right to control Luis' life.

What if something happened to him?

The usual pretext, a mother's pretext: *I was worried, you don't think about us waiting at home when you're out.* Does Luis think about you when he's out, does Luis think about you when he's with another woman, does Luis think about you when he lets loose inside another woman? Do you think about Luis when you're with Andrés? Yes, you think about him, you think about Luis particularly when you're with Andrés. Guiltily, suffocatingly, you think about Luis, as if you owed somebody something.

No, not somebody, you owe yourself something. Peace. You owe yourself peace. Why are things so complicated? How can people live so calmly, people supposedly fall in love only once, don't people, don't other women sometimes feel like making love with someone else? And what do they do then? Forget it, put up with it, endure, carry on as if nothing were happening? If you do it too often it will become a habit and finally you'll build up a tolerance for it.

You can't, you don't want to.

Then why this anxiety? You don't want to or you can't? Inability. You can't believe it. You simply cannot believe that nothing happened. You don't want nothing to have happened either. Nothing. What? How much would be too much? Are you too childish? Perhaps it's immature to go to bed with someone and fall in love. Things need to be kept separate. Maybe that's adulthood.

But you loved Luis already, you always loved him. You didn't fall in love when he touched you, you didn't bind yourself to him when he exploded inside you, it was the other way around. The red sweater, you look for the red sweater, the smell of perfume from the other day is still on it, it's a day to dress in red, day or afternoon, since the day has almost passed. It was because you were in love with each other that you went to bed together. Not the other way around. No, not the other way around. At least the day is moving forward. At last. At last, it's almost over, the time to go meet Andrés has arrived. No sign of Luis yet, he hasn't called, no trace of him. It has started getting dark and you'd better get moving if you don't want to be late for Andrés. The red sweater. He'll surely spend the whole weekend with Elisabeth. Red. Women, women's bodies and colors. As you go down the stairs, you say to yourself that women dress to please men but to make women admire them, and you're happy with the sentence. Sentences, think in sentences. High heels. *The sound of your high heels as you arrive at the metro station.* The world of women. Seven thirty. Take the metro. Nussdorfer Str: 7:45 pm. Yes, better take that one. The next one will arrive in ten minutes. Too late, ten minutes too late. There's nothing like a good fuck to give you a crush on someone. That's what they say, at least. So what.

The heat of the metro, the close smell of the metro stop, people hurrying, that rushing mass of strangers. There's a black woman in front of you. The end of white Europe. You're happy, as if those who want to maintain whiteness were against you, you're happy that the woman in front of you is black and she'll have kids, lots of kids. Maybe not, maybe she won't have kids, maybe she doesn't want to, maybe she can't. The window reflects your misty image back to you. You can't see the streets from the metro windows because the train went underground a few stops back. Once, about fifteen years ago, you were on the bus on your way to San Sebastián, happily looking at the green countryside around Deba. You saw all of life's doors open before you. Maybe. Maybe that's why you were so happy at that moment, a happy oversight. Now you know that with every door you pass through there's no turning back, it becomes impossible to pass through other doors, each choice has its price and can't be taken back. You're happy that the woman sitting in front of you is black, black and much better looking than the young chubby man, soft and white beside her. You're happy, but you also feel sorry, something makes you feel sorry. The woman must make you feel sorry. Yes, she makes you feel sorry for her and you wouldn't want to be in her place. You wouldn't want to be a poor black person among the Europeans of a still very white Europe. Blacks, blacks who die of hunger by the thousands in Africa, black children. Mission Sunday, the small piggy banks. *Finish what's on your plate, God will punish you, what a nuisance you are, so many children dying of hunger in the world, and what God gives you, you leave to get cold on your plate.* God gave to you while killing African children with hunger, what he took from the African children he apparently gave to you, to the little white girl, that disgusting piece of meat getting cold on your green and white duralex plate must be what he took away from the Africans. Why did God have to take from some, from others, to give to you, to you, who weren't hungry in the least. Wasn't God, as Madre Columba used to say, omnipotent, all-powerful and all-knowing?

The metro has arrived at the stop by the cathedral. Stephansplatz: 8:13 pm. You would happily stay on the warm train, sitting opposite the beautiful serious black woman, but she's getting off too and you cheer up. It's windy outside, and cold. Springtime cold, springing to summer. Summer and summertime aren't the same thing. When you were little, they said summertime. Then you learned it was more elegant to say summer, it was better.

Like when you learned to write the letter H in Basque words.

But summer and summertime have never seemed the same to you. Like grandma and grandmother were also very different. One you loved, the other frightened you. When you learned to write H, you thought for the first time that springtime could be a time for springing. But that didn't seem to make much sense.

Better, yes, to wait in a coffee shop. It's cold. A large coffee shop on a small street. Above the door, *Café*, like in French. *Café Engländer*. A few tourists, there's always a tourist, someone or other around the expensive shops near the cathedral. More, though, in the big streets. This coffee shop must not be in the guidebooks. This café.

A thousand faces, a thousand sentences, a thousand smells, a thousand dreams spinning around in the world. It seems like all of them are there now in the *Café Engländer*. Andrés hasn't arrived yet and you choose a small table in the room farthest from the bar. You order a large beer and look at the plain fat woman at the table closest to you. Then, while you look for your cigarettes in your purse, you look at the man with the fat woman and then at a man in a suit at another table who looks like a yuppie. Linearity, a fruitful encephalogram, but flat. You see how the girl opposite him explains things to him, how sure she is, how she masters her subject. What is she talking about? Work, soccer, culture. You don't care, you'd bet it's all superficial, giving her opinions with no emotions, no trace of doubt. She disgusts you. A fifty-something woman closer to the bar is putting on a brown leather jacket. Black pants, low-heeled shoes and a well-maintained body. The soft chin of the man who must be her husband judging by the way he helps her on with her jacket, his pudgy belly, disgusting. Again, disgust.

Saturday, 8:30 pm

Andrés sees you immediately when he enters the *Engländer*. From far away, almost from the door. You're seated at a table way in the back. There's less light in that part of the café.

You're putting out a cigarette, slowly, in the glass ashtray. You don't see Andrés.

Andrés, as he enters, in the first second of his first glance, sees that you're getting old. He notices your age in the way you look at your cigarette and in the skin of your cheeks. Andrés hasn't touched the skin of your cheeks for a long time. Maybe for years. And he doesn't feel like touching it either. Andrés suddenly feels sorry for you. You seem like an aged doll to Andrés, a little girl whose skin has thinned. He'd like to hug you. To hug you without touching you.

You don't see Andrés arrive and come over to your table. A quick kiss and a nice smile, that way of smiling with his eyes, Andrés' own way of smiling. He says something about how hot it is in the café and orders a Campari from the waiter who brought you your beer, a Campari with orange. He takes off his jacket and pushes up the sleeves of his sweater. Andrés' red hair and strong arms covered with freckles. Something makes you think of your grandmother's home, the light in your grandmother's house in a corner of the hall by the kitchen on a spring afternoon. From there, as if by osmosis, you move on to the home of your great-aunt, who lived in the apartment above her. Can there be osmosis in the world of memory? You remember the magic of that childless old couple's house. The otherness. The fascination.

"Some places don't exist anywhere anymore, they're gone forever. It's not possible, it's not physically possible to return…" You realize after starting the sentence that you're speaking aloud. Andrés doesn't raise his eyes from the drinks menu in his hands. "It's very sad," you continue, looking toward the window.

"What's so sad?" says Andrés in a monotone, but lowering the menu in his right hand he places his other hand over yours.

"That some places are finished forever. I was remembering my grandmother and my grandmother's house, aunt Fermina and uncle Julián, they were my mother's aunt and uncle really. When I was little, when I got out of school, we sometimes went up there for our snack. They had a big box of buttons under the kitchen cabinet."

You stop looking at Andrés, from the feel of his hand you can tell he doesn't care what you're talking about and, under the pretext of tapping your cigarette ash into the ashtray, you take your hand out from under his. You get a lump in your throat when you think of how well you got along with your grandmother and how proud your grandmother was of you. Your grandmother used to say you had to get the best out of life.

You don't say anything more.

You start gathering up the coasters that were spread out on the table. They aren't all the same shape. Some are round, others square. It's not easy to gather them up, and you start to arrange them by shape, but your thoughts flee and, jumbling the coasters in your hands, you see your grandmother shuffling the crazy eights cards. You can't believe your grandmother is dead, that you won't see her anymore, that you'll never again play crazy eights together. It seems to you, involuntarily in some territory beyond reason, that you'll be able to visit her when you return to San Sebastián and your grandmother will be there at the kitchen table, waiting to play crazy eights with you.

Saturday, 11:00 pm

Luis is on his way home. He can't find a parking place. He went around the block twice and finally had to leave the car quite far away. Shit. *Scheisse*. Bad weather, a harsh wind and no parking places. It seems to Luis that the world has turned against him, today the world has turned against him. He can't get Elisabeth's anger out of his mind, Elisabeth's anguish. Today she let out what she must have been keeping silent for years. Where did Elisabeth get so much anger? Luis saw a different Elisabeth, a hard Elisabeth he didn't recognize. He was almost frightened by Elisabeth's voice, untouched by sadness.

No, not frightened.

It shut him up.

For his part, while Elisabeth was talking to him endlessly, he felt a burning need to get away from her. While Elisabeth threw it all in his face, the hatred she had built, amassed, cultivated, nurtured for years. How many years of hatred could it be? Three years? A couple? Did Elisabeth hate him only this last year? Only for the last few months?

Why had Elisabeth called him? Is this why she called him at his office on a Friday, is this why she called him away from his reading, his peace? Is this why she stole his chance to spend Friday evening with Andrés and you?

He wants to see you. He'll tell you everything. He has to tell someone and that someone is you. You'll understand, you'll explain it, you'll console him. Like before. Like that time on vacation when you were students. He wants to hug you. He wants to touch your perfume, your detachment. Where is his key? Now he can't find his key, that's all he needs. No, it's in the pocket of his raincoat. One of these days he'll lose it, the openings of his raincoat pockets are too wide and he flings the coat around every which way when he takes it off. He should put it in his pants pocket.

It doesn't look like anybody's home. He opens the door to your side of the house. There's no light to be seen, nothing to be heard. You must have gone out. What did he expect? That you would be waiting for him? Is that what he thought? Is that what he wanted? That's what he hoped. Definitely, yes. On the verge of admitting this to himself, he decides to turn on the computer and work.

Sunday, 12:05 am

The last metro home. The last metro. *Le dernier métro*. Catherine. *Belle de jour*. Teresa, Teresa who can't quite make it, living the anxiety of someone just barely catching the last train. Teresa. You.

There are a lot of people waiting for the last metro, but since it's the first stop, you get a seat. When you sit down, you hold onto your husband's arm and put your head on his shoulder, softly, looking for shelter, asking for shelter. You know he won't understand, but he'll like it and, in the end, that's what it's all about, pleasing each other, understanding is the least of it, full understanding. Will. Faith. Faith and will. The will to have the faith to move mountains.

When you arrive home, Andrés opens the apartment door slowly; it's late.

The glass door between the two sides of the apartment. It's open. You could have sworn you closed it when you left, so that Luis, if he returned, would find it closed. Now it's open and Luis' black jacket is on the sofa by the entrance.

Farther down the hall, a weak light from behind a door that's slightly ajar.

You are happy, unbelievably happy, you feel like laughing. Your drowsiness has disappeared. If he weren't alone, he would have closed the door all the way, and besides, the light is coming from the study, not the bedroom. He could be in the study with someone, with a woman, with Elisabeth. It was in a study, after all, in your study on a winter afternoon, that the two of you started this phenomenal mess. No, you know he's alone, the door is a signal, a call. Everything falls back into place, like on weekends until now, were the only woman around.

You don't dare go to Luis without bringing your husband into the game.

"Look, our prodigal son has returned," you murmur as Andrés helps you off with your raincoat. He doesn't say anything. Or you don't hear him say anything. On your way down the hall, it seems to you that he smiled. That Andrés smiled.

"Hi, we're back," you say putting your head through the crack in the door.

"No kidding!" Luis doesn't know how to hide the tenderness of his smile in words, he always has to say something silly. He has the computer on.

"How come you're home so early?" you ask him, reining in your desire to go in and kiss him.

"And you? You have less of an excuse. When it comes down to it, I'm just a lonely old bachelor. If I can't find anyone to pick up by midnight, better to retire. After that, you won't get anything but a headache"

If you couldn't see his face, you'd think he was angry. He seems tired, but not mad, maybe a little sad. You find the nerve to approach, but you don't touch him.

"So you don't think I should be sitting at home then?" Luis adds, less grumpily. "It's not like I have great things to do out there, to tell the truth. Besides, I think I caught a chill and my stomach's a little upset. What have you two been doing?"

You don't like it when Luis uses the plural to ask you something, but what else can he do? You look toward the window. It's dark out and the window is a mirror. Yes, you were right to wear that skirt. "We ate out. At that new restaurant in the museum. Quite good," you say, half to Luis and half to yourself in the window. You're quiet for a moment. You look very small in the dark glass of the large window, again you lack strength, but you like it, that woman dressed in red and black has something about her. What?

"What?" says Luis.

"What what? I didn't say anything," you say, startled, looking away from the window. You don't want to ask Luis what you wanted to ask him, but you can't just say nothing. "Do you want to come to the living room? Andrés and I thought we'd have a nightcap." Now *you're* using the plural, deliberately, like a safety net.

"Maybe you two would rather be alone..." he can't think how to go on.

"What's wrong?"

"Nothing, shit, nothing. Don't pay any attention to me. I don't know what's up with me either." Then he adds, "I got mad at Elisabeth. Well, she got mad. She told me I didn't like her, only my image of her. That I was in love with myself and my own reflection." He gets up and grabs you around the waist with both hands. "Why didn't you marry me?"

You bite him on the nose to close the door on something that's breaking inside you. "Because I suspected what Elisabeth told you. Let's go to the living room."

You walk down the hall feeling the nearness of the body behind you. The temptation to walk faster. The desire to flee from that body's nearness. When you enter the living room, Andrés greets Luis and starts talking about something he read in the newspaper. You cross the room to the cupboard where the drinks are kept. You turn your head to ask Luis what he wants, you're leaning over the open cupboard, you're opening your mouth, you have the sentence ready in your mind, but you don't say anything. You see the two men wrapped up in their conversation about the newspaper, one standing, one in the armchair. In the end, you say nothing. Besides, didn't Luis say he had a chill and an upset stomach? You'll have a whiskey, blended, a blended whiskey, a smooth whiskey, the bottle closest to you.

When you stand up, Luis looks at you. Andrés is walking toward the bookshelves and Luis is looking at you, answering Andrés politely, but looking at you and smiling. A new smile you don't like on his face, an overconfident, seemingly complicit smile, his too-moist lips swollen by the craving in his eyes.

Maybe if Andrés weren't in the same room.

Maybe if he weren't talking with Andrés about the newspaper.

But you don't want Andrés not to be there, you want him there, you don't want to be alone with Luis, with this Luis you don't recognize, with the new Luis, with this Luis abandoned by Elisabeth.

No, he's not new. He's not totally new. When you were students, remember? By the balustrade on the Concha beach, the two of you were looking at the sea, in the harsh wind. It must have been a holiday when Luis was studying in Madrid. A holiday or a long weekend. He would come to San Sebastián then. It must have been something like that. Those green pants of yours. Yes, it must have been summer, or it was warm at least, those were summer pants.

Luis was telling you about a liaison he had had in Madrid. Sometimes he told you about them, you didn't know why exactly, but back then you assigned whatever intentions you wanted to people's actions and were happy with that. You drew the world to your liking, to your taste. Back then, the world was as you saw it from the window of that bus to Deba. You wanted to take Luis' telling you about his affairs as a sign of friendship, and that's how you took it, that's what you told yourself. Or at least that's what you tell your present self. Who knows how you felt about it then? You don't know for sure. You really don't know.

Or you do. What is memory, finally? Weaving together what stays with us. Mending tears. We don't really remember. We fabricate what we remember, remembering is fabrication, to understand, at least to make a story that can be put into words from the bits that remain in our brains. Weaving without meaning to. Wanting to understand, taking up a new thread. Unthinkingly.

You have one of Luis' entanglements in mind, the one he told you about by the balustrade on the Concha looking at the sea.

He took a girl home on his motorcycle after a big party. There were big parties then. They had been dancing and the girl was really coming on to him. Luis was hot for her and pleased that the girl let him take her home, but that's as far as it went. When they got to the girl's house, she said goodbye and thanks and went through the doorway to her parents' house without giving him so much as a lousy kiss. That was the first time, and the most vehement, you ever heard someone called a *cocktease*. You thought it was funny or at least that's what you led Luis to think. That's what you think now. You remember that and you hate yourself. Cocktease. You didn't like the look of Luis' face toward the end of the story. He was looking toward the sea, but he wasn't looking at the sea. He also didn't look at you the whole time he was telling the story.

Andrés has found the book he was looking for and while he's looking for the page, Luis goes over to him. An atlas, or at least a fat book with maps in it. Luis takes his wet stare off you and you remember the glass of whiskey in your hand. You sit sideways on the end of the sofa. You stretch out your legs and rest your head on a cushion, almost lying down. You don't feel like drinking. To tell the truth, you don't feel like being there, you don't know why you brought together in this room the two men who are looking so interested in the map. You're tired, you want to go to bed.

If you keep this up, you'll have circles under your eyes tomorrow and the wrinkles around your mouth will be deeper than ever. You don't like your face much lately. Are you sick? Same old ghosts. The last time you went to the doctor, he told you he saw no reason to worry. Take vitamins. Take it easy. Work less. No reason to worry. The doctor told you. Sleeping less is natural as you get older, you sleep less and your sleep is lighter. That's why you're tired, not enough sleep.

But your case is extreme. You're no spring chicken, but you're not all that old either. You're between thirty and forty, that's not old yet. And you don't have that many worries either. So why the nightmares? So many nightmares. So bad, so scary. When you do manage to sleep, you have bad dreams. Death and sickness. You wake up sweating in fear. Same old ghosts. It must be the pills. The pills they gave you to sleep.

Other less frequent side effects may include fatigue, dizziness, dry mouth, dyspepsia, confusion, agitation, speech disorders and depression.

Besides, there's the thing about your periods, but that may be because you've lost so much weight. Why have you lost so much weight? How much? Maybe not so much. You notice it with some of your clothes. Andrés and Luis haven't said anything to you about it. Luis doesn't know how you were before. Andrés maybe doesn't remember. There's nobody else close to you.

Luis and Andrés are bent over a map. You, lying down, in your corner of the room. No, at that time the border between Austria and Hungary… You don't give a damn what they're talking about. Do they care? You hear them from afar, as if your body is there but your mind has gone to the kitchen, to the kitchen to drink a glass of water and then to sleep, to sleep without brushing your teeth. Close your eyes and sleep. Close your eyes and go away. Go. Go to sleep. Drowsiness, sleepiness, let sleep take you, let it take you in its arms.

Did you brush your teeth, honey? Yes, mom.
Yes, grandma. Yes, I brushed my teeth, will anyone
come with me to say my prayers? Baby Jesus
just like me, you're a little child. I have a heart
and it's for you, take it, take it.

Take my heart, but leave me
to sleep in peace, to sleep alone, to cry
alone, will somebody tell me
sad stories with happy endings,
so I can fall into the arms of sleep with a smile.
I've had enough of sad endings for
happy stories.

Schloss Belvedere. A palace. The imperial
gardens, the effect of spring, the warm smell
of green grass. A young mother playing
with her little child, running and jumping, trying

not to let the automatic sprinklers
wet them. The sweetness of the mother's voice blends
with the round laughter of the child.

Ojalá mi madre fuera así de feliz conmigo,
I wish my mother had been that happy with me, when
I was a child that little, her
little child, when I was her toy. *Ojalá mi madre fuera feliz.*
You don't know how to say that
in Basque, to say that like that in Basque. The form
determines the content. We are servants of style,
slaves to words.

Nevertheless, that's the only thing that can be done.
Tell, speak, talk, change feelings into
words, turn them into words. *The only possible*
intercourse. That's why old people like them
so much, people whose life is almost
used up, talk, tell, speak.

When there's no partner for conversation, he who
suffers or feels excessive pleasure talks
to himself. To suffer, it's not possible to
suffer excessively. Suffering, like
death, has no measure.

As in San Sebastián, spring in W. is allowed almost
no time in the leap from winter to summer. Rain,
endless rain. The streets are dressed in gray glass by the
endless boundless rain.

The sun of the Belvedere gardens doesn't shine
on the street where you are. You don't know how you arrived
at these streets, these sunless

streets. The changing light must have brought you. No,
nothing brought you. There you are and the sun
has turned to rain and, then, the clean light
of a small, tidy, private clinic.

An enormous table fills the whole room and
a dark-haired doctor is on the other side of it.
On the other side of the table. On the other side of the room.
Far away. You're very small and you know that soon
you will die. That's why you're there. You don't
know how you got there, but you know
it's because of that, because soon you'll die, that you're there.

You see the words coming from the doctor's lips
in chains of letters,
flying toward you. The doctor's words
will kill you. You know it. The terrifying
words loosed from his mouth, turned into letters.
You know it. That's why you can't move from your
place.

The doctor's voice, without words, isn't
coming from the doctor's lips.
The doctor's voice, without words, fills
the entire space of the room above
the enormous table. No more voice can fit
in your ears.

Your head will explode. You can
not flee. Your eyes are bound
in the chains of words hurtling toward your heart
from the doctor's lips. Those words, those words
saying soon you'll die, must reach
your heart. You know it.
Your death comes written. The doctor has the results

of your analysis in his hands. Not on paper. It's something
that looks like stone. You know it's written
in German. The doctor's words are in
English and the whirlwind that fills his voice, the room,
your head, is terrifying.

You're very small. You'd like to be
in the Belvedere gardens with your mother, with the water, playing.
You know it. But you won't move. You won't
wake. You won't leave that world where one can
go from the Belvedere
to the clinic without doors.
It's terrifying, you must die, but
mothers play with children under the Belvedere
sun, in the spray that waters the gardens.

Summer
Uda
Sommer
Eté
Verano
Udara
Raumarti
Amaŕ
Grisma
Xiatian
Natsu

Sunday, 9:00 am

Bells are ringing in the first warmth of the summer morning, there's nobody on the paved streets and you feel that life is passing you by. Naglergasse. Sunday. The bells cover the sound of traffic from streets farther away. You have the results of your analysis in hand, in your pocket, warming and wrinkling in your right pocket, folding tighter and tighter under the nervous movements of your fingers.

Apparently there's nothing wrong with you. It's all in your mind. That's what they tell you. In your mind. Not in your body. Everything is all in your mind. All caused by your nervousness. Everything, in your mind. The mind is not the body. The soul. The soul is the mind. Pain of the soul. Body and soul.

Relax. Take a break. What do you have to take a break from? What is making you so tired, if you don't do anything? You came to W. for that reason, to relax.

With your husband. To your friend's house, your old friend's house.

Apparently, you haven't relaxed. No. You know you haven't relaxed. You haven't had a break. Is there such a thing? Where? A break, a real break?

There are many eighteenth-century buildings and you think that those buildings were built at some time, those large stones put prominently one on top of another, so that people could live there, so the maids could go out for milk in the morning, and the men to work, through the giant doors of the entranceway, saying good day to the neighbors. The children would have run to school. You don't know why (images from films?) but when you go back in time in your imagination, you always imagine children in groups and running. Now a lot of those buildings are used for offices and, in the still morning, the smell of death stands out above all others downtown. Offices, malls, small clinics and laboratories. The antiseptic smell of those places. The clean, paved streets.

France. Many foreign cities look French. That must also be memories from your childhood, since foreign in your childhood meant the south of France. That area of France was the Basque Country, the Basque Country but so foreign, so different. There were Basque flags on the streets. The first Basque flags you ever saw. Women with scarves on their heads riding motorcycles. Clean white narrow sidewalks. Then there were the shops, so many different kinds of yogurt and new potatoes in orange mesh bags and soap that smelled better than on your side of the border.

You don't remember about the duralex, the green and white kitchen plates you hated so much were smuggled across the French-Spanish border before your time. Your grandfather and your mother must have bought them before she got married. Your mother, before her wedding, that young woman who was not yet a mother, who would later be your mother. That woman who was younger than you are now. That woman did become a mother, she who was not yet your mother. The results of your analysis. The statistics of your body are on that warm paper you fold over and over, a piece of your truth, the ratios of your chemistry. Everything is OK. The constituents, the substances of your blood, of your urine, are within normal limits. It's hard for you to imagine your mother before she was your mother. To help yourself imagine her, you try again to grasp the fact that your mother, that woman, when she went shopping for plates with her father before her wedding, was younger than you are now. But it doesn't offer any reassurance; all you do is lose the thread, the paper in your pocket fills your thoughts again. You're OK. You should feel OK.

Often, too often, you remember the dream in which the doctor told you you were going to die. It's been weeks since you had it. You don't remember all the details, but the memory is very vivid. It's hard to believe how real some dreams seem. How much they stick in your mind. How they remain hanging in your awareness, coloring everything else that happens. As if they really happened. You're too young to die. You woke up saying that. That night you didn't sleep much. Nor many other nights, lately. These last few years.

You don't want to think. You'd like to leave yourself behind. Forget your dreams. That one dream. And other similar ones. They told you there was nothing they could do. The doctor's impartial face, his well-maintained skin. Maybe it wasn't like that in your dream. You're surely confusing him with the real one, the one who did your analysis. It was too late to operate, the doctor in your dream said. He kept telling you, over and over. Maybe with a year-long treatment, a treatment started right away. He kept repeating it in English, as if it weren't enough to have said it in German. A couple of months at most before the pain would start. In English, with a touch of a German accent, in English. *One or two months.* The voice came to you from far away, echoing, bouncing off the clean walls of the examination room. The door of the examination room far away, at the end of a bright white tunnel. Far away. *One or two months.* You understood it in German too. You waited, however, all your senses quiet, hoping that the English version would be lighter, or holding back the certainty of death for a second by instinct. You waited, because the door was too far away.

Forget those dreams. The worry will make you sick. Truly sick, finally. You recite that refrain over and over again to yourself. But worries don't come from dreams. It's dreams that are born of worry.

And if it did happen? What if the results of your analysis really were as bad as your worst dream?

What would you do if you knew for sure that you would die soon?

You have often asked yourself this question. You started a long time ago. On the way to the convent school. On the bus. What would you do? What would you do if they told you you had only a few weeks left? Until today you had no answer, no real answer. Until today you never asked, really asked that of yourself.

Dare.

With no pretense of illness. Without the justification of your analysis. Dare to do something total, make the coming time yours. Don't think about work. Don't think about your husband. Don't think about your family. Nor your town, your places. People. Don't think. Do. Move forward. Or backward. Forward or backward. Move.

The hotel in Genoa. The whiteness of the walls in the examination room melds into the flowers on the walls of that hotel. That's the answer, the real answer to the question. You want to be in that hotel, you don't want to be anywhere else, your body wants to be there. While the fright of your sudden decision leaves you gasping, you think of the hotel and it brings you peace.

The stone faces look out at you from the façades of the buildings. All those faces watching from the walls. Watching you. Looking without seeing, watching you as you walk down the clean sidewalk. Then also watching you as you go over the pavement. Looking without seeing. Why do they put so many faces on the walls of buildings? Lion faces, men's and women's faces. Some seem sad, a few are laughing, many others don't show anything, they watch. They just watch.

How lucky to be able to watch without showing anything, without feeling anything. You'd give a lot to walk without feeling anything. Without feeling bitterness, without envy of happiness, to walk, just to walk. First one leg, then the other. First put one foot on the pavement, then the other and like that, keep on going, keep on living. You look around, seeking shelter from the confusion you feel when you start to worry about life, about time and biological ties, about ties of love. You're going toward the river. You're going away.

Maybe they're waiting for you at home. Yes, you should go back. When you reach the canal you'll go back on a different street, on some street with fewer faces on the walls. Most likely up the steps that lead to the synagogue. Yes, you think that area is nicer. Maybe Andrés and Luis are having breakfast. You find that the thought makes you nervous, involuntarily you start wondering what the two men would talk about to each other when you're not there. You're walking faster and faster and you feel utterly foolish when you realize that you're out of breath.

The two men are old enough to manage on their own without you, and besides, they knew what they were getting into when the trip was planned and the one offered his house and the other agreed to it.

Did they know?

Does anyone know anything, when we say we know the future and accept it? Do you know what you're getting into, where you're going, what will happen to you? Maybe you yourself are the one who doesn't know how to manage on her own. You don't know. You don't know, but you want to, you want to try, you need to. What God sends us may be a test and we just have to learn to live with it. Madre Columba. Where is Madre Columba now? Where is Madre Columba, where is God? To test, tests. Tests and exams. See what's happening, but you yourself see it, feel it, in your body, not in someone else's movie. In your own, in your movie, you realize that the camera has started rolling. You feel life passing you by, like a cold shower on your skin, like a violent penetration into your guts.

The Turkish newspaper seller smiles at you, you think. What those poor people go through in this white, expensive city! Heartache. Although you wish you could have their health, their peace. The others, all the newspaper sellers, and the poor little old lady you felt so sorry for, who checked the price of sugar ten times in the supermarket, they all seem full of tranquility to you today. All but you. The Turkish and Indian newspaper sellers on the streets, the poor little old ladies, Luis, Andrés. Everyone. Everyone else. All the men in your life. Is Andoni OK?

Andrés at least, yes. He's OK. Andrés' strength, Andrés' attractive roughness, lost passion for Andrés. Andrés, your man. Andrés' sturdiness. It seems like he's always been there, he's always been your man, you've always been married. No, when you were at the convent school, at Madre Columba's, you weren't married. Andrés wasn't there, but he was on his way, wasn't he? Yes, he was on his way. He was ready. That's how the script read. While Madre Columba's was preparing you for life's tests, Andrés was backstage, waiting for his scene to begin. And you, from the stage, you saw Andrés. Andrés or someone like Andrés. A husband. Almost ten years with him, his wife. Almost more than ten years, almost a third of your life. From the time you finished the preparation, your whole life. Your whole adult life almost, plus the earlier promise: the husband watching you from backstage who would step forward when his scene began. Andrés.

You want to see traces of misfortune in the glances of those who pass you in the street. Doubts and fears.

Luis is not your husband, he's not anybody's husband, he has never been anyone's husband. Luis is not your husband but he is something to you, he is something of yours, something not new. You've known Luis for ages. You were together for a couple of years at the university. At the beginning. Before you went to different places to get your degrees. But even then, you still wrote to each other and saw each other most holidays in San Sebastián, especially during summer vacation. You used to go to the beach early in the morning to run and swim, until the beach started to get crowded. Luis always had a girlfriend, but neither you nor he thought it of much consequence. Sex, yes, you talked about sex in general and in the abstract. Pseudo-literary, pseudo-scientific conversation. Everything overcome, no problems. You also went to bed together a couple times, one right after the other, on the same weekend. Like paying off some kind of debt to each other. No big deal. You were better at talking about it than doing it, you at least didn't enjoy it that much, but you thought you did. At the time you thought that was just the way it was. Silly. Well, you enjoyed it a little, with the confidence of the first touch, with the power of the first kiss, with the deep love of the first shared sweat. Then what happened? You saw each other again, but you didn't go to bed together again. Maybe you didn't know what to do. Maybe he didn't know what to do with you. You paid your debt to each other and that was it. What debt?

You know that in your life there have been those who didn't know what to do with you, who didn't dare to make a decision, not even a Saturday afternoon decision, those who couldn't bring themselves to even make arrangements to go to the movies and you, always, you forgave their cowardice. You took the blame yourself sometimes, head bowed. Like when you said in that fax to that green-eyed guy from the mountains that you would be in his town the next day. The interview you had to do would be over by noon, but you probably wouldn't make the noon train and you would hang around seeing the town until afternoon at least. When you were typing, it seemed to you that you were underlining the words *at least* and you smiled a cunning smile internally, to yourself. You had often daydreamed about an erotic escapade with that guy from the mountains. To tell the truth, it would have been enough for you at the time if he had taken your hand to laugh together before the monument to the local Basque flute player.

There was no laughter, you didn't see any monuments, green-eyes didn't so much as touch your hand, the green-eyed mountain man didn't answer your fax. He didn't show up at the main entrance of the city hall either, when you finished your meeting that gray mountain noon on that sad Saturday.

You still feel alone now. Like at the damp noon of that town, wanting to open your umbrella in the middle of that grayness and looking around to see if your mountain man would show up, unable to give in to despair while you calculated that you were missing the train. You're alone and it feels cold even though it's summer. You're alone and you don't know what to do, try to catch the train or let it leave you behind this time too, while you open your umbrella. Damned men. There have certainly been a lot of them who didn't know what to do with you. Plenty. More than a couple, a lot more.

What was that other guy's name? Pedro. That time you found a book by his favorite poet, sent it to him wrapped in red, special delivery on a gust of wind from your heart, with a little note that looked like it had been dashed off quickly. *I thought of you when I saw this book in an old bookshop, of you, because you saved me from suicide by talking about this poet just to me in the throng at that dinner party. Will we have another opportunity to talk about poetry and blah blah blah.* You received no answer at all. Your heroism received no acknowledgement whatsoever.

You ran into Pedro again at another thronging dinner
party and he sat far away from you. He gave you a foolish
smile around dessert time and came over to you at last in
the cordiality of after-dinner drinks. Because of his tone
when he thanked you for the book, and because now you
were sure that he had gotten it, you were hurt very deeply
and you wanted there never to be another such occasion.
Anger and shame mixed together. God, oh God, how
could I ever have felt tenderness for that man?

At such times your insides harden and you regret ever
having opened the door. They didn't know what to do and
they ran away, but not forever. Later they came back, hidden in the crowd, using work as their excuse, with drunk-
en desperation. They didn't know what to do with you.
Then. Them.

Did you? Did you know? Now, at least, you don't
know. Now you're the one who doesn't know what to do
with you, who doesn't know what to do with yourself,
with yourself, with your body, with your rotting insides,
with your malady. You've lost the key. You don't understand. You don't know what to do. Maybe you didn't
know before either.

You knew how to begin. You started things off. You
thought you were starting to build bridges. Giving love,
asking for it. But when they didn't give it to you, when
they didn't give you what you wanted, what did you do?
What have you done until now?

You took the train. You took the train after the one
you deliberately missed and went on as if nothing had
happened. As if nothing had happened.

You waited for the next dinner party. Waited for the
next thronging dinner party. To see if you would find
what you wanted in the next man who spoke to you of a

poet. What you wanted, what you still want. What you want.

You have no way out. You have nothing to do, no exit, no direction. But you have to do something, you have to exit somehow, you have to go somewhere. You don't want to end up waiting now too. Life doesn't stop just because fear demands it. You have to go somewhere, to some other place, you have to flee incessant time. There's no other way. Time won't heed your fear, it won't stop, it won't stop for you and you also won't stop it. Here at least, you won't stop it, if your life is someone else's here too. Here you have no right to take away all that belongs to time, its fencework, its field, its work. Here you'll have to go on, continue, no matter what the cost, live, exist, move forward, endure to the last. Walk without direction, go out without an exit, do things without having anything to do. Waiting for that thing you want from other people. Like until now, like always, go on. As if nothing had happened.

Like you did when you returned from Genoa. Fifteen years ago. Go on. As if it didn't matter. Tied to the daily grind, go on.

Go. Go away. A change of place. Leave the place that defeats time, your time, go far away, flee the time that knows you. Go, go alone, to a place where no one knows you, go to another place, to a place where time doesn't bind you, go to a rootless, anchorless place. Then, at last, maybe, time will be yours and you'll be able to do what you want to do. Let it be in your hands when your body's time, this malevolent maddening time will end. You'll be alone but you'll know what to do. Without informing anyone, giving no reason, asking for no explanation, just you. In someone else's unknown place, you'll borrow a piece of cruel time belonging to no one and that piece will be enough for you to rest at last.

Sunday, 10:30 am

The door to the street seems heavier than ever to you. Oh moon of Alabama. The stairs tire you. Go up slowly. Under the Alabama moonlight, the moonlight, the moon light, the monthly light. Monthly, your monthlies. Are the dead of Alabama at rest? You like that part of the song, where it says *Oh moon of Alabama*. You'd like to be able to sing the whole song, to be able to sing with that woman's voice. The people downstairs must have the record on. Ute Lemper. You have that record too. Ute Lemper sings Kurt Weill. We must die and we need money and we need men.

When you put the key in the door to your side of the apartment, you feel something like responsibility inside you, and with it, the desire to free yourself from blame. Voices come from the kitchen. Anyway, when it comes down to it, you know that it's because of you that the two men are together in the kitchen. In this kitchen, in this house, in this city, but not in this world, not in this life, not forever, not essentially. You are the tie. You are the knot that must be undone. You, your body, the bridge, the umbilical cord between the two men. The two men, talking with each other, wanting to impress each other, wanting to amuse each other. And you, between them. In the meantime, you are your body, the results of your analysis, that's what you are, that's your future, your body's conditional future, the present of your body's health.

Or not. What doctors look for, they find. What they don't look for, they don't find. This sickness of pure sadness is what's keeping you from sleeping. The nothingness of boredom is what has dried up your monthly blood. The impossibility of love is what has caused this pain in your lungs. You drown in the mire of your soul, which is not overcome by the limits of your blood tests. So they'll be unable to name what's happening to you. There is no diagnosis. But you don't believe it. You don't believe what's written on the paper, because you're inside your body.

You will not unfold the paper.

What if you closed your mind like that too?

Hanging over you, the desire of the two men, which doesn't touch you. A deeper impulse rather than desire. The homosocial desire of heterosexuals. That hidden need even greater than acquaintance, insatiable curiosity. The curiosity that Luis and Andrés feel for each other, the curiosity that leaves you out. They know you. They've gone to bed with you. With you, with your body. That's what you are, your body. You've gone to bed. They know you. And that's it. That's all. End of story. They haven't gone to bed with each other, they don't know each other. There's something they don't know of each other. But with you, they've crossed the bridge and they didn't reach you, but they think they did or they don't care. There's nothing else to be done though. It would be better if they were gay. They would look at you from the distance they would keep from women and that, the distance and the look, the awareness, would please you. Or if they were misogynists. You would feel like the main character. The homosocial desire of men. A woman's body as something to be explored, something to be conquered. A hunter's trophy to display to one's peers, to other males, other equals.

You're festering. You're looking for excuses. Looking for what the doctor didn't give you. Wanting to gather the strength of hatred.

When you reach your bedroom, you'll take the paper out of your pocket so it doesn't fall out. No one must find it, you yourself don't want to see it again, you don't want to read it again. You'll put it inside the small zippered pouch inside your large suitcase, you'd see it every day in your toiletries bag. No, you'll put it in the pouch in your suitcase, you don't use it for anything else. It will stay there as it is now, scrumpled into a little ball, unread, but with you just in case. Wherever you go, you'll have the scrap of paper nearby. You don't believe it. You don't believe it, but there it is. The license to oppose your fear, your great fear. The source of strength to defeat your smaller fears. The will to go far away. The courage to flee. Or the need.

One day what the scrap of paper promises will be true. Your body will have no fatigue.

Or a lie: then there will be another paper, another document. A diagnosis. One that names your malady. The label hidden beneath the last label. A real explanation. Now it has no name. It's not yet time.

"Hi, it's me!" you say loudly as you walk down the hall toward the kitchen.

"We thought you'd gone forever," answers Andrés, smiling, standing by the table. He's holding a coffee cup.

"It's not that easy to get away from you two." You wanted to hide your nervousness with the tone of your voice. It didn't come out the way you wanted and you feel almost embarrassed, as if they had caught you, as if they could see your secret plans, which are becoming stronger and stronger within you. Childishness. There's no chance in this world, everything is a game of probability.

"Andrés and I had started planning to go out cruising for chicks," Luis is carrying a basket of fresh-baked bread to the table. As he passes you, he gives you a kiss on the cheek.

"Hey, I won't stop you." You want to appear calm but you don't know if you're succeeding.

"With you by our side, we don't need anything else," Andrés seems very relaxed as he says this and something like peace rises from your neck to your nose. Luis smiles at you and puts your coffee down in front of you.

No, they don't know anything. But how could they have found anything out if it's all new to you as well, you don't even know when you decided. You don't know exactly what you decided, but you see the hotel in Genoa in your mind and you know that you've decided to leave. You decided just a little while ago.

Maybe today, when you went for a walk with the results of your analysis in your pocket.

Or yesterday.

Or the day before yesterday, as soon as you saw the doctor's face. His well-maintained face. His thin lips, saying first in German and then, slower, in English, like in your bad dreams: *ein paar Monate, one or two months.* As in your dreams, a month or two. Take it easy for a couple months or so. The easier the better. Sleep a lot. More pills. Stronger, with these you'll definitely sleep. *Ganz sicher.* If there's no change, come back. They would do more tests. The doctor's address is also on the scrap of paper with the results of your analysis.

Or yesterday, when you went for a walk along the canal, or at that metro stop, when you were imagining

yourself falling under the train. Not even doctors can protect you. No explanation. You're alone, you alone have to
make the decision. Once and for all, decide. Break away.

Maybe coming to W. was the first step. No, don't fool
yourself. You came to W. to solve things, to take a break.
But you didn't get one. You found Luis in W., forgotten
Luis, lost Luis. In W. you lost Andrés or you dared to lose
him, dared to accept that you lost him. Or else he lost
you. He's lost you, though he may not realize it. You realize it. You've thought about it. You've learned it. Now you
know and because you know, it is so. And now you want
to forget them, you especially want them to forget you.
They'll be just fine without you.

Think.

Think again and again until you figure it out. Repeat
it until it sinks in, until you learn it by heart. Two times
two, four. Two times three, six. Two times four, eight.
They'll be fine without you, even without you. They'll be
fine. It would have to be like that, it has to be like that,
anyway. Let it be like that. At least you know, you're sure
that you don't want any of their sympathy, you don't want
them to be sorry for you. Or you can't induce that. You
don't know how. Doctors didn't help you either. You have
to find a way to go away quietly. Go away without saying
anything to anybody. No goodbyes. No tears. No tears
from anybody.

"What's the weather like out there?" Andrés' light
voice brings you out of your thoughts. He's standing, coffee finished.

"Quite chilly, but it looks like it'll be nice. It'll get
warm around noon. We should go to the zoo, I'd like to
see the gorillas." As soon as you say it, you're surprised by
what you've said.

"That means you're on the rag or you'll get depressed at any moment." Luis must be thinking about the trips you took to the Madrid zoo. He knows the gorillas upset you and the ones in zoos make you sad.

When you need to cry, your strategy is to go see the gorillas, like watching a sad movie. You're not especially sad now. Maybe too sad, too down to be sad. You want to visit the gorillas, a last visit to the gorillas of W. Besides, it will be hot, the stink, you think of the stink of the animals' cages, think of the children, family outings on Sundays. Even so, you want to see the gorillas.

You need to cry and can't. You have no tears. You have no tears left. Do tears get used up? But you haven't cried many of them. You must not have had many. A woman of few tears. A hard woman always running from decisions. Hardened.

"We could eat at the restaurant inside, couldn't we? It's very pretty, very decadent," you say to persuade the others.

"And very expensive," says Luis immediately.

"That way there'll be fewer children."

"Richer children, maybe," adds Andrés.

"They're quieter, they're raised better." You don't want to lose the argument.

"You're such a snob," say the two men at the same time.

"So are we going or not?" You start to raise your arms to underline your despair.

Andrés answers you with an affirmative smile. Luis is drinking his coffee and puts on a gorilla face. They love you too much. What to do with this love? What does anyone do with love? What can be done? Suffocating. They should stop it, they should stop this inconsiderate love for you. They should take a real child to the zoo. Maybe sometime, some Sunday, they'll take a little child or two to the zoo, and a happy wife.

A man always has time, all the time he wants, all the time in the world to become a father. Not women. Not you, Teresa. You know the time is approaching, is approaching you, for a final decision, for a final no. A cliff. A leap with no return. A bound. A boundary. Endless, a fall, speed increasing due to the weight of your body. Start getting old without children. Fast, start getting old very fast. A leap without any support. To leap without a net. Peace at last. Accept unmasked solitude. Embrace it. We're all alone, each in his own hole, waiting for the end.

Sunday, 12:00 pm

When you leave the house, Luis locks the door with his key. You always leave this task to him, respecting a sort of hierarchy. As he starts to go down the stairs behind you, he remembers the phone, the answering machine. He doesn't know for sure whether he left it on or not. Elisabeth. If he were alone, he would go back, but he doesn't want to make you stop, or maybe he doesn't want to have to offer an explanation. He could say it was for work, but it would be a lie. Elisabeth is the reason, the reason for his worry about leaving the answering machine on, the explanation for his desire to turn back. Maybe the answering machine is on, anyway.

Luis' confused need to see Elisabeth. His desire to have word of Elisabeth. A desire difficult to define, an amorphous desire. A dry desire that doesn't even give him the strength to call her. She, Elisabeth, should call him. Or even better if they ran into each other. Where does Elisabeth hang out now? If she were at the zoo, it would be hard to bump into each other. It's too big. Besides, Elisabeth doesn't like animals much.

His need for Elisabeth. The consolation you didn't give him, the dependence you didn't cure, the support he didn't find in you. Does the anger of that night still endure in Elisabeth? Weeks have passed. Is she the former Elisabeth again, the usual sweet Elisabeth? And what if she called and the answering machine wasn't on and it made her so mad she didn't call again for weeks...

The results of your analysis have left you totally alone. Alone. More than ever. More alone than ever. If you at least had the excuse of sickness. If only they had told you what to do in writing this time too. If the script followed naturally. No. You're alone. Accept it. Once and for all, finally, accept it. Believe it. Look at your solitude, look as closely as you looked at the corners of your eyelids a little while ago in the mirror, when you were doing your eye make-up. Your solitude.

The fatigue of pretending not to see, the impossibility of hiding your head again and again, worn out by the pain left by holding onto the loves on your journey so tightly that your fingernails bleed, the craving for solitude of a wounded animal will carry you down the empty streets, and if you refuse, you will have no time to grow old. If you dare to go away, maybe you will also dare to grow old.

This time Luis can't tell you his troubles. It doesn't look like you want to hear anybody's troubles. You seem odd to Luis, you seem to have nothing to do with the Teresa who came to W. That was someone else. That was someone closer to the Teresa he knew before, when you were young. You haven't even been in W. a year, but it seems like ten years have passed. You've aged, or a piece of a Teresa he doesn't know has emerged. He doesn't find it strange that you go out walking alone. You did that before too, a long time ago, when you were students. In fact, you often ran into each other on similar solitary walks of yours in San Sebastián. On those occasions you either talked a lot or almost not at all. But you always seemed especially sweet, especially serene, to Luis. Now when you return from those walks of yours, you almost never talk a lot. Sometimes you try, but it's obvious you'd rather be alone, go to your room and lie down. You must be tired. You told them you have writer's block. Luis doesn't know if he should believe it.

He doesn't know if Andrés has also noticed it, if he's guessed anything about you. He would like to confirm with someone that he hasn't just made it up, but he doesn't dare to talk to Andrés about you, to talk about you in particular.

Andrés has to find at least a little time for work today. Otherwise his week will be thrown completely upside-down, he thinks as he takes your hand on your way down the stairs. You suddenly seem especially fragile to him and he tries to feel guilty about his work worries. You almost always want to be alone lately and he can't miss this opportunity to be with you. You talk less and less. You don't seem to pay much attention to Luis either.

You go for walks at all hours and you don't want anyone to go with you. Just the day before yesterday, when you were dressing to go out, Andrés said he was about to go out too, maybe you could go together. Your nervousness seemed way out of proportion to him and you came up with excuses not to go with him. He insisted, it was a pretty area around the offices where he would have to be and he would finish what he had to do quickly if you wanted to wait for him. Even so, you didn't go with him. That night he didn't dare ask where you had gone. You frighten him more and more, that whatever-it-is around you, that something in your accusing look. Luis is also treating you delicately. At least that's what Andrés thinks.

Sunday, 12:30 pm

To get to the zoo, you have to take the number 58 tram. Strassenbahn 58. Strassenbahn. Street-train. The W. zoo is at the Schönbrun mansion, at the palace. At the entrance, there are huge greenhouses with palm trees and butterflies. The one for the palm trees is bigger than the one for the butterflies. Palm trees are bigger than butterflies. Some princess at some time must have walked around happily among the butterflies. Did she walk around? Did she walk around happily?

Luis and Andrés go ahead of you talking about the architecture of the pavilions and gardens. Luis, Andrés, your men, your friends, your loves. You want to see them like before, the nostalgia of an earlier you, of you as you were, burns in your chest. You can't. You can't return to the past, you can't be who you were before. You don't desire them. You would like them without sex. Hugs, sexless heat. Some people, other people, don't make a mess of their love lives, even the bond of sex must be an easily released attachment of limited duration for them. You have solid knots inside you, the years you've lived, all of them, have opened for you, you have them all in your gut somewhere, one on top of another, each hanging from the edge of its own knot.

Knots, lumps, they hurt you when you breathe and you're tired.

Very tired.

No, perhaps those things that hurt you aren't knots but holes, holes in the pieces of your heart that you left behind for every friend, for every dream, for every lover, for the most insignificant, for one-night stands, even for every hour. Your strength gushes through those holes. You're bleeding your desire, your desire to go on.

How to cure the wounds left by loving if not by escaping? But how can you escape fear, if not by paths of love? How to love, then, without healing those wounds? How to love if your body is so tired?

Sunday, 1:00 pm

Luis sees you in the middle of a mass of children, stone still, looking at the mother gorilla.

The baby gorilla wants to play with its mother, but the mother doesn't want to and tries to get the baby off her. You bend down.

Luis looks at you again.

Bending over, you're at the same height as the gorillas sitting on the other side of the glass.

Smiling, you're bending over, smiling bending over. You don't seem to want to leave at all. Aren't you hungry? You hardly ate breakfast. It makes Luis want to touch your shoulders, your back, your waist, your neck. Between you and him, children.

The noise of children around your silence.

You want to free yourself, free yourself from the others, so no one will see you, you want to lick your wounds unwitnessed, without an audience, to lie down and gather strength without acquaintances, or lie down forever. For the others to free themselves from you, take you out of their way. You'll put yourself in God's place, ruling the fate of those at your side. Let your fate not be his, let it not color Luis' and Andrés' future. You'll go in search of a new land, toward a sweet language and the warm Mediterranean light. You can't manage in your language, in your languages. These lights have become too cold for you.

You're not well, it's not something they told you about someone else, at the moment you're one of those people who become statistics in reports on depression. You want to go on alone, go on as long as your body will endure, go to the Mediterranean, to Genoa. And no one will make a film about your pain, your anguish.

Dolly back is what film-makers say when you pull the camera back and widen the angle to the point of losing the actor in the distance. Lost in the wide angle, melted into the background, you'll have to spend the next part of your life alone and on your own. It's not good for anybody and you'll try to make it so no one gets hurt. Sadness, like death, never serves any purpose. Your sadness and death, at least, are worth nothing to anybody. Or are they?

Eternal rest they say at funerals in churches. Eternal rest is death, a true rest. But only God can give it. He alone can give rest because he alone gives work, suffering, inability. Life. Only he who gives life can take it away. There is no other rest. Life belongs to the one who gives it an end. It is his. Not even this is yours. Life, the only thing we truly possess. Borrowed. Nothing more. Not even the only thing we possess is really our very own. For women, for you, the most prized possession was virginity. You lost your virginity in Genoa. You lost many virginities in Genoa. Dolly, boom, dolly, like a toy dolly in English. That girl who was so happy at the bus stop at Itziar died in Genoa, that doll who adjusted things to her liking. It ended there. You returned from there a woman. Now you want to return there.

The singer Fabrizio de André is also from Genoa, was from Genoa. No, he's still alive. Isn't he? Yes, he's alive, otherwise you would have heard. If you die first, he certainly won't find out about it, at least not unless you drop at his feet, and that's unlikely. The fruits of fame. The fame his voice deserves. Better, anyway, that no one should find out. Is there any insurance that pays without letting anyone find out? Changes of identity and such things are fine in movies, but they're too much work in real life. It would be great to go to an agency and pay a certain amount of money so that if something happens later on such-and-such a trip, please arrange things so the body doesn't rot in the streets or so that the local officials of an unknown place don't work in vain, but take care that nobody finds out. Dolly back. Deal with the paperwork, sign the necessary forms and documents. Bury the body quietly and neatly, but don't say anything to the family, please. Don't let anyone find out. Amen.

It's queer how out of touch with truth women are. They live in a world of their own, and there had never been anything like it, and never can be. It is too beautiful altogether, and if they were to set it up it would go to pieces before the first sunset. Some confounded fact we men have been living contentedly with ever since the day of creation would start up and knock the whole thing over.

JOSEPH CONRAD, *Heart of Darkness*

You didn't mention anything about your analysis to Luis in the café, in
your café, in the café you'd never been in with
your husband. What for? You spoke little.
You only ruined things,
but you wanted to be with Luis for the last time.
It was something like seeing the gorillas,
but the gorillas didn't ask you for anything, the gorillas
didn't ask you anything, they didn't even
look at you, only that female gorilla's
indirect glance, but you're not
sure if she was looking at you or if she looked
in your direction because of
the piercing shrieks of the little children. Luis was not a gorilla.
Luis suspected something and asked you
what was going on with you. He didn't believe you
were leaving open the option of returning
to him. He must have guessed from your voice
that it wasn't true. He didn't understand, he didn't want to
understand why, if you had made the decision to leave
your husband, you didn't start living with him right away.
Sometimes, yes, he said he understood and
it seemed so, that he understood your desire to be
alone, but right away he started saying if you
left his side you'd regret it
and go back to your husband.
Why do men, all men, all
the men that you know, think
if you don't want to be with them it must be
because you want to be with someone else? When he told you
to stay with him, taking you by the hand and looking into

your eyes, you had a lot to build,
to invent, to invent together, you had to see
if things between you worked as well as
you dreamed, then something
flooded your insides, something melted
inside you. What had Luis
dreamed, how had he imagined your
life without Andrés? He was sorry
you and Andrés were breaking up. It seemed to be true,
you had no reason not to believe it. He appreciated
Andrés after the time
you spent together and he had made no effort
to break up your twosome, he accepted his position
in second place, he knew it well, but
now, when his path was clear, he wanted to work
to bring you close to him. For a moment
you felt the temptation to tell him the truth. The
temptation to tell him part of the truth. The prettiest piece of the truth,
if truths have pieces. Can a piece of the truth be said
without saying the whole? Isn't it the whole truth
that you're leaving because you love them? You've even
forgotten why you're saying goodbye,
why you made the decision to go away.
You're forgetting that you're sick. Again
and again, you remember as soon as you forget.
You're disgusted with him, with
your husband, with his desire, with your
inability. Then you realized that he was getting
angry and you tried to be happy, happy
because he was getting angry. You didn't tell him you thought
all relationships end up
the same way, it wasn't worth it to begin.
You didn't want to leave him unhappy, you didn't want
to recreate in Luis the expression of despair
you saw in Andrés.
What do you know about me, Andrés said to you without

looking at you. He'd go back to San Sebastián
to wrap up a few things at work. He'd take a look
at the house, at your house. If possible,
he'd close it up again. If possible,
he'd continue the work he started in W. for another year
at least. Most likely in Brussels. He had
the opportunity. You knew, in any case, how
to find him. He would always wait for you. He didn't
understand why you had to separate.
He respected it. He had to respect it.
You didn't know for sure if you detected
calm as well, under that despair, under his
sweet words. You think so, you think
there was also a little calm. You don't know
for sure yet if he believed in the finality
of your decision to leave. Do you
believe it? You prefer anger, Luis'
anger, to Andrés' despair. All right,
they'd get over it, anyway. They'd find
someone. Men manage. In couples
that separate, it doesn't take long
for the man to get together with
another woman, especially when there are no children.
They'll find someone. Luis too will find
someone, beloved Luis, beautiful Luis
will find another woman and will be
happy. Maybe he'll remember you
sometimes and he'll understand that this escape
is the last stage of love, of love
for him. The biggest.

With your head against the dirty window of the metro, Luis'
last hug comes to your mind, again and
again. You couldn't speak, it was difficult
even to take a breath,
you thought the urge to cry would

smother you. You hated that café and
the tree on the sidewalk, the tree next to Luis'
hug. You say to yourself you'll
never again pass by there, you'll
never enter another café like that one, you'll
never again hear that language around
you. You're going.

You don't want to think, you want to stop
the images that flood your mind, the endless
painful memories. How long this
last metro seems to you, how much time
the doors need to close when other times
they seemed so fast.

Solitude and living without love and
not knowing what to do about it. That will surely
be the direst illness. One with no name,
but one that can kill you. If there's no exit,
better not to know it. Better to believe that there is. Or
that the best you can have is what you have,
and things as they are. That there's no need
to seek an exit. To tell the truth, you have a lot, much has been
good in your life. But you want something else.
Tell the truth. Tell yourself the truth.
You don't have enough, it doesn't satisfy you. Better not to know.
It would be better for you not to know. But it's too late
for that. Maybe there is no other way,
maybe this time there's no turning back and it's
over. Things aren't like you thought near Itziar
on the bus from Deba to San Sebastián. You can't
retrace your steps, can't go back along the same road.
Even if there's nothing else, what has been done is finished,
it's over, and, knowing that, you know it forever. You
won't be able to forget. Things didn't look that
hard, that permanent, the time you were on the Deba bus

going to San Sebastián. Then.
Now you're on the W. metro going to the train station.
Südbahnhof. Times like these are cut
in films, shortened at least, nothing
worth seeing is happening. The character packs
his suitcase, like you did an hour earlier at
Seegasse 16, 3rd floor, right, choosing
what to pack quickly and clumsily. The next scene,
if there is such a scene, and especially if it's on a train
or bus, tends to be very short, what needs to happen
happens in a few minutes. Otherwise,
the spectator must be entertained
with what the character is thinking about or with
what other characters are doing, if he's not to get bored.
But this time you're not a spectator, you're a
character, and you don't want to amuse yourself
with what's in your own head. Maybe for the first time
you know that you're the main character in
your life, maybe at this very moment you're
nearing the end of your life as a spectator. The game is over,
the present is really happening, you're
going downhill and you want a light to fall by,
the better to see how you're falling. At least
you don't want to feel cold. If the body is
extinguished, let there at least be the sun's light and warmth.
To light the body, the smell of the sea.

From the metro to the train, the long train hours. Pills and
mountains, people all over the place. The train
will carry you and you'll see
how things are left behind. Towns
and people, mountains and rivers. Behind.
Like memories. They filled a place in your
life as you did in other people's lives; now you're going,
you're going forever. Leave others in peace, as
they leave you, alone and empty,

full of memories. You're going. Piercing the landscape,
passing to the other side at the speed of the train,
mountains and rivers, towns, toward the sun,
toward the Mediterranean, in Genoa, maybe in Genoa
you'll get off the last train. Genoa,
De André's city, the incomprehensible dialect of Genoa.
You don't want to think, let things pass
through you, you want them to cross through you. Open.
Open your body and your mind. Pierce
your insides, let them endure, images and memories,
landscapes and faces you know,
let them pass, let the wind carry them away. In
one hole and out another. Let those
that go in one hole come out of the newly opened
hole. Without causing pain, in one
and out another, softly, as softly as a man's penis
withdraws once it has emptied and shrunk,
without notice, leaving behind only a wet softness.
Soft sweet memory erased like the
landscape in the window. You're happy, you
feel light, you're not hungry, only
thirsty, maybe you took too many pills with
only one glass of water. On the train
there's that car where they sell drinks. You'll buy
water, it's best not to drink alcohol with medicine.
It occurs to you that it's funny to call
sleeping pills medicine. To cure what?
Sleeping pills cure the lack of sleep. Sleeping
is the cure. Thus, when you sleep,
you're healthy. But that doesn't matter much
now. Above all, there's the fact that you don't want
to drink alcohol now, you don't want to. You
feel good, in the pleasure of a still deep sleep.

You rest your head against the windowpane,
as on the bus from Deba to San Sebastián,
maybe when you were passing by Itziar, when you

were twenty. At the other end of the car an attractive
young man sits down. Since when
do you find young men attractive?
Well, maybe he's not that young, he's got
a bit of a beard. Thirty years old? He's not that
young. Younger. Younger than you.
Like Imanol from work, younger than
you. Imanol. How far away from you
Imanol seems. Since when do you take note of men
who are younger than you? Since you started getting old,
since you started the second half of your life,
maybe. Downhill. Since you felt the fear
of time. Don't be afraid.
You'll be happy. You'll be fine. Don't
be afraid. Be afraid. Fear itself.
Be fear. Fear. Fear is
you, it doesn't come from outside, be at peace
with fear and you won't feel it. That's what we are,
our fear, our fear and our
fantasies. That's what we're made of. The things
we know, the things we remember, the things
we don't remember even though they happened and the things
we dream about that never happened. All this creates us.
This is what we are. What we love and what we
hate, the color of our eyes, our body,
our pains and pleasures, the smell
of our mother's hands when we were little. What we think we see
in those who look at us. In those who look at us,
in other eyes, in others.
The desire of younger men. The rhythm of
our breath and the beating of our heart. Our
most secret dream and the way we tell
stories. The dryness of our skin and wetness of
our eyes. Our fatigues, our more and more frequent
fatigues. Our old and new wrinkles. This is
what we are. This is it. To unite all those distinctions,

occurrences, characteristics of a thousand levels,
a thousand dimensions in one place, in one
body, for them to come together once
and for all. In your body, in
your life, throughout your body's
process, from the beginning of your life to
its end. Happen. Occur. Life.
One's own life. One's own. You. Happiness.
For each person to do his own thing, manage to do it.
For that it's important to know what you
want. What do you want, what do you want
from now on? To each his own.
Happiness. Manage to do it. Fill life and
fill it intelligently, without causing misfortune
to anyone else. Without causing
misfortune, it's not about asking for someone else's happiness,
no one has the right to hold another responsible
for his happiness. Happiness cannot
be given. Each person is responsible for his own happiness.
Do no harm, cause no pain. Escape.
Hide. Escapes, the breaths necessary
to keep on living, the poisonous messenger of
one's own or someone else's servitude.

Landscape, journey, the overwhelming
blue of the sky.

The flowers on the walls of that hotel and the heaviness
of those curtains, the light trying to come in through the
partings.
From the farthest corner of the tunnel, from the end,
the color of Andoni's eyes, the strength of
Andoni's voice, of that voice, the strength
of young Andoni, your certainty
when you were younger, the belief
that you gave him your untouched self deliberately,

the consolation that everything that remained to you would end up in him. The beginning again, the wholeness of that time, the security of your beliefs; for your fears, a remedy.

E se vai all'Hotel Supramonte e guardi il cielo
tu vedrai una donna in fiamme e un uomo solo
e una lettera vera di notte falsa di giorno
e poi scusse e accuse e scusse senza ritorno
e ora viaggi ridi vivi o sei perduta
col tuo ordine discreto dentro il cuore
ma dove dov'è il tuo amore, ma dove è finito il tuo amore

Grazie al cielo ho una bocca per bere e non è facile
grazie a te ho una barca da scrivere ho un treno da perdere
e un invito all'Hotel Supramonte dove ho visto la neve
sul tuo corpo così dolce di fame così dolce di sete
passerà anche questa stazione senza far male
passerà questa pioggia sottile come passa il dolore
ma dove dov'è il tuo cuore, ma dove è finito il tuo cuore

E ora siedo sul letto del bosco che ormai ha il tuo nome
ora il tempo è un signore distrato è un bambino che dorme
ma se ti svegli e hai ancora paura ridammi la mano
cosa importa se sono caduto se sono lontano
perchè domani sarà un giorno lungo e senza parole
perchè domani sarà un giorno incerto di nuvole e sole
ma dove dov'è il tuo amore, ma dove è finito il tuo amore

FABRIZIO DE ANDRÉ, *Hotel Supramonte*

And if you go to the Hotel Supramonte and look at the sky
you will see a woman in flames and a man alone
and a true letter of the false night of day
and then excuses and accusations and excuses, there's no going back
and now travel, laugh, live, or you are lost
with the discreet order in your heart
but where, where is your love, but where does your love end

Thank heaven I have a mouth to drink with and it is not easy
thanks to you I have a boat to write on, I have a train to miss
and an invitation to the Hotel Supramonte, where I saw the snow
on your body so sweet with hunger, so sweet with thirst
this season too shall pass, doing no harm
this subtle rain will pass as pain passes
but where, where is your heart, where does your heart end

And now I sit on the forest bed that by now has your name
now time is a distracted man and a sleeping child
but if you wake up and are still afraid, give me your hand
what does it matter if they are fallen, if they are far away
because tomorrow will be a long and wordless day
because tomorrow will be an uncertain day of clouds and sun
but where, where is your love, but where does your love end

FABRIZIO DE ANDRÉ, *Hotel Supramonte*